By A. G. Mojtabai

ORDINARY
TIME

—

DOUBLEDAY

new york   london   toronto   sydney   auckland

ORDINARY
TIME

a novel

—

A. G. Mojtabai

Published by Doubleday, a division of
Bantam Doubleday Dell Publishing Group, Inc.
666 Fifth Avenue, New York, New York 10103

Doubleday and the portrayal of an anchor
with a dolphin are trademarks of
Doubleday, a division of Bantam Doubleday Dell
Publishing Group, Inc.

Library of Congress Cataloging-in-Publication Data
Mojtabai, A. G., 1937-
Ordinary time / A.G. Mojtabai. –1st ed.
p.   cm.
ISBN 0-385-26416-X
I. Title.
PS3563.O37407   1989
813'.54–dc19   88-34873
CIP

ALL RIGHTS RESERVED
PRINTED IN THE UNITED STATES OF AMERICA
SEPTEMBER 1989
FIRST EDITION

BG

for my parents
NAOMI *and* ROBERT ALPHER,
who have taught me much about faithfulness

A pagan once asked a rabbi: "Why did God choose a bush from which to appear?" He answered: "Had He appeared in a carob tree or a sycamore, you would have asked the same question. However, it would be wrong to let you go without a reply, so I will tell you why it was a bush: to teach you that no place is devoid of God's presence, not even a lowly bush."

—MIDRASH

VI. Ordinary Time

43. Apart from the seasons of Easter, Lent, Christmas, and Advent, which have their own characteristics, there are thirty-three or thirty-four weeks in the course of the year which celebrate no particular aspect of the mystery of Christ. Instead, especially on the last Sundays, the mystery of Christ in all its fullness is celebrated. This period is known as ordinary time.

44. Ordinary time begins on Monday after the Sunday following January 6 and continues until Tuesday before Ash Wednesday inclusive. It begins again on Monday after Pentecost and ends before the first evening prayer of the First Sunday of Advent.

The missal and breviary for Sundays and weekdays in this period follow the same plan.

—POPE PAUL VI, APOSTOLIC LETTER MOTU PROPRIO: APPROVAL OF THE GENERAL NORMS AND THE NEW GENERAL ROMAN CALENDAR

Ordinary time is the unceasing human effort to balance quicksilver on a knife.

—FR. STEPHEN FOGARTY, O.S.A., LETTER TO AUTHOR

CONTENTS

Enter Fleeing

"I told you already. It says: 'Take a bow.' See the girl in the picture? Doesn't she have a nice dress? See what it says: 'Be nice.'

"Look, I don't want to read. Can't you let me think? Let Mommy think. All right, just this—

" 'Take a bow.' Sit down. Sit down! Stop squirming if you want me to read to you–

"Forget it–you're a pain in the neck. Eat your apple. Watch it. That's Gramma's present. With you it won't last more than a minute. See this? Judy and Freddy are on a seesaw. 'Up and down, up and down!' You like that? 'Judy is up, Freddy is down. Freddy is up, Judy is down. If Judy is up, is Freddy down?'

"What's the matter? You want to teetee? Do you? Then stop jiggling around. Why don't you lie down? Mommy has to rest for a while. Shhh . . . Just shush. For five minutes.

"Honey, don't do that. What did I tell you? Don't eat the pits! Eat around the pits. You're bugging me today.

"I'm tired. Can't you leave me alone for five minutes? Five crummy minutes? I'm going to eat your nose—

"Come back here! You want to color? Don't be fresh. Here—make a picture for Gramma. Make a face, make a face for Gramma. She doesn't know you know how to make a face. Here's the paper. Here. Don't spill the crayons. I'm going to give you such a smack. No, I'm not going to draw. You do it for yourself. You do it! Oh, all right . . . just this once. Here's your face. See the ears?

"In another minute I'm going to smack your head off. Can't you do anything for yourself?

"Anything. Make colors. I don't want to color. You color. Gramma wants a picture from you, not me. You know what . . . Let's lay down for a while? Just a few minutes. You wanna lay down? . . ."

Seems like he's been cooped up for days. The same bus, airless, the same voice never letting up. Same forsaken stretch of emptiness as far as the eye can reach.

"Of course, you don't know how to draw a princess— you never tried!"

He stares hard out the window. There's nothing out there but empty land sliding by, nothing to mark off one mile from the next, except now and then a bunch of whatsis—how do you call them?—those cam-and-lever things for sucking up oil . . . Grasshoppers—that's it—exactly what they look like. Most of them are stalled, but one's nodding.

"You don't know how to draw a princess because you always make me do it!"

SLOCUM. They're going through a town. Stoplight, gas station, grocery and Dairy Queen—they call it a town.

"Honey, do you want me to put the crayons away? No, I don't want to draw. I want to take a nap. You can color. You're a big girl, you can do it. Just try—

"Okay—Mommy colors the dress. Mommy colors the hair. Red. Why is it red? Because I feel like it. I don't want to color.

"All right, that's nice. Snuggle up. I'll color in a little while. You lay down. No, in a while. I don't want to color. I don't want to. You color for a few minutes. By yourself, okay? And in a little while, after I'm rested, I will.

"Honey, lay down with Mommy, okay?"

He keeps his head turned to what's passing outside. Nothing again: red, clenchy soil, a few poor trees leaning the way the prevailing winds have left them. Somebody back of him says, "I like scenery on calendars best." He wishes he had a headset to drown out the voices. Can't take much more. Must be a stop coming up. How many hours?

This it?

WELCOME TO CLINTON

HUB CITY OF WESTERN OKLAHOMA

Hub city? This? A wide and empty main street, the

traffic lights slung between two posts, rocking, clanking in the wind.

Fine, he's ready. Let it be this. Can't wait: he's standing in the aisle before the bus is in park. The door heaves–opens with a whoosh–

–so eager he can't remember whether he's going up or down. The last step is a lurch, he didn't know it was the last. Solid ground, but he sinks down, almost to his knees. A slow, billowy bottoming out, loose as stirred mud. Better hold it.

Sign on his left. Feet seem to know the way, when something seems– Not wrong, but not right. This–house? –room?–hall?–it's nowhere. It's not friendly. The wrong floor, he thinks, but that's crazy–there's only the one floor. Something's inked up his mind. He can't remember what in hell he's doing here, what state, what town, what country in hell this is–

Could be concussion.

He can't remember!

Starts back the way he came, when–*wait*– At the sight of the bus, he stops dead in his tracks. It's the bus he came off of, he's sure of that. See? Marked LOS ANGELES, where he's going. His hands feel numb, clumped; fingers webbed up like they're stitched together. He stares at his fingers, tries to spread them. *Push–push–*

Not a flicker.

Your answer is you don't know? Your answer is you don't remember?

Fagged out, is all. Pulped. Breathing in all that car exhaust. He says his name: *Val.*

Val–that's you. *Val*, me, *Val*.

The brat goes by, riding her mother's shoulder, leaning way back, staring at him with smiley upside-down eyes. His right hand's tightening, making a fist, a knot—
    He'd like to punch out her lights!
    Walk fast, walk fast, he tells himself, his heart racing, feet at a dead stop. But—there!—that does it— Anger's sprung the lock, like always, magic for him. And nothing's tied. His fingers ease loose of themselves. He can spread both hands—they're fine.

    Feels like he's eaten his name off the birthday cake and he wants to move now, wants— Where to? Where he'd been heading. It will take a minute to refresh his recollection exactly where that was.

    He asks for two bowls of chili and helps himself to all the crackers he can hold. His hunger is a deep well. It irks him to be paying for food when he'd stocked up on everything. He'd been sleeping and eating in the car and, as he traveled, had laid in a store that could keep him going for days. Someplace over the state line he'd stopped for a lube job. That would have been New Jersey—or Pennsylvania. Was it? Or was it farther on? He's not sure. Maybe outside of Pittsburgh? It seems to him that all those bridges came afterward . . . But maybe not, that part's a blur.

    And the rest is all jumbles. He remembers only this terrific push and toppling sideward, and—where was the steering wheel?—the rearview mirror winking at him from someplace down under. Then, at the sound of liquid seeping, the smell of gasoline, kicking, throwing his weight against the bashed-in door until it gave. The diamond spray of glass underfoot, beautiful in an eerie way; his head splitting with pain. He'd been lucky, though, damned lucky; the car was totaled, but his legs still worked; he'd managed to salvage his suitcase and clear out. Kept on hustling down the highway, imagining the screaming red flashers gaining on him, till he hitched a ride to the nearest Greyhound and continued heading west.

His head still aches from the windshield but he has no bumps or bruises. Only this little tiny cut on his lip, he had to look twice to make out. Bone's thicker than glass, after all.

"Mind?" It's an old man in peachy pastels–pastel shirt, white pants, white sneakers–settling his tray. "I don't like eating alone," he explains.

Two desserts, Val notices, no main course.

"Chili–," he says, shaking his head. "Makes my mouth hurt just to look at it. I don't know about chilis–they're devils, them little peppers, those dark green babies worse'n the red ones."

Val doesn't feel much like discussing what he's eating. That doesn't set Old Pastels back any, though. "I've done nothing all day," he confides. "I step off the bus and my shoes are tired already. You going far?"

"California," Val says and yawns into his bowl.

"You're a young man, you shouldn't be tired. If you're tired out now, think what you'll be at my age. Where'd you start from?"

Val considers first the question, then the teeth of the man asking the question. The teeth seem more important. They're brown or greenish, depending. It's how the light hits them. The old man's staring, waiting, his spoon lifted. Val's about to answer, "You were asking–what were you asking? What were we talking about?" when the man says, "I just got back from Nassau–Fantasy Island. Ever been there?"

Val shakes his head.

"Nicest people in the world."

"Eager for your money, are they?"

"Only way they can make a living," says Old Pastels. "With bananas fifteen cents a dozen, coffee thirty-five cents a pound."

Val wipes cracker crumbs from his lips and takes a long swig of water. Soon Old Pastels is handing around photographs of his wife. "Wonder-ful woman!" he says. In this one she's wearing the dress she was buried in. It's pink. When he passes the photos to the man at the next table, Val seizes his chance and scoots for the door.

It's too early to get back on the bus, too late for a real walk. He still has ten or fifteen minutes to kill, so he wanders through the gift shop, eyeing the state plates, the Indian sand paintings, the cactus jellies, and the model windmills made out of tongue depressors. Trash! There are bagfuls of rattlesnake eggs stashed next to the register. Lumps of paste, probably; the bags are sealed.

I loved what I bought . . .

Waiting for the boarding call, he paces in the sun. When the call comes, he takes a last lungful of free air and mounts the steps.

Pretty soon they're on clear highway again. Broad and flat and oiled with light. The two across the aisle from Val are silent at last; the brat seems to be sleeping, her head flung back; every once in a while, though, he thinks he sees her eyelids lifting. Soon other voices are crackling all around him. Old Pastels asking, "Where are we now?" and somebody answering, "Can't help you there." Then somebody back of him talking nonstop about the Russians. "The Americans are afraid of the Russians and the Russians are afraid of the Americans. Well, and see? No, it isn't. No. It isn't politics at all. It's metal. It isn't atomic bombs. It's metal. Believe it or not, it's still true. And I'd say the same thing in the tallest building in the world. This is the age of metal. There's something in the met . . ."

When he wakes, the light is everywhere. He's been on this bus forever, it feels. He remembers the crash as something dreamed, one of those headachy dreams. The man at the wheel has been talking for some time. There's someone, a young man, riding the steps. Must be a driver, too.

Still in Oklahoma, but they can't be far from the Texas border by now. Middle of nowhere, by the looks of it. The red soil is fading, the few trees are fewer. They pass a trailer drowned in high grass, an idle rig. "Time's hard all over," the man at the wheel observes. "You see that?" He's talking to the man on the steps, but Val, too, strains to see where he's pointing. Looks like a general store. "Owner died about a year ago." The place is shut: door and window boarded up. "They just sealed it. Nobody's done nothing. Candy, Coke's still in there. Wonder how long the fizz can last . . ."

Dirt blowing. And tumbleweed, whole bushes of it, wind spirals, whirling down the road, hitching on to bumpers, latching on to fences, to anything, anything that passes.

They pass a mesa, dotted with green scrub, a shallow canyon. A riverbreak, dry and threadlike.

He wonders at the hand-lettered sign:

RATTLESNAKE

EXIT NOW

He stares at another blankly:

DRIVE FRIENDLY

The road smooths out. A grain elevator looms up in the distance, the only thing to look at in miles.

The brat is leaning over the aisle now, poking her face into Val's face, like she's listening with her eyes. He keeps his head to the window. Nothing to see out there but a haze of heat and dust. His head lurches toward the glass. He is stuffed with sleep . . .

And then they're braking– He opens his eyes in time to catch a fringe of city skyline in the distance, a city that looks to be just resting on the prairie.

Val has never seen a sky so big. So rinsed with brightness. Unshadowed, except for a distant worry line of small, rumpled clouds that seem to be hurrying away from him.

Traffic ahead.

The roads come together here; real traffic, the first since Tulsa. A billboard on stilts. In colors of fire:

HE IS COMING AGAIN

IN GREAT POWER

AND MAJESTY

The city has broken into chunks and hollows. More like a town, really. What Val saw scratched on the horizon turn out to be three buildings wearing their names—the Santa Fe, the Texas National Bank and Ferris Petroleum—towering head and shoulders above the single and double-storied, but making scarcely a dent in the sky above.

"Folks." The driver's picked up the intercom. "This is Durance. Durance, Texas."

The Everlasting Arms

They have forty-five minutes in Durance. Enough time, Val figures, to breathe and stretch his legs. At long last–

Fresh air!

Grand Street is deserted. He can look clear down to the end of it to where the prairie begins, where street turns to highway, then to shimmer, the blacktop blue and watery in the sun.

Not a soul.

Maybe he's dreaming, walking in a dream. There's nobody else walking. The banks, offices and parking lots are empty, the stores shut up tight; it's after five. Not what you would call a bustling town. The signs are up for clearance sales, for leased-and-moving-out and every-thing-must-go sales. Whatever's happening here happened a long time ago.

He likes the glaze and the emptiness. Light floods the windows of the shops and blackens them, making them secret in broad day. To discover what's inside, he has to make a visor of his hand and peer under it, leaning his face to the glass.

WILLY'S LUBES SHOCKS WHEELS ALIGNMENTS . . . Yes, it was just outside of Pittsburgh where he had the lube job done. He passes the used car lots. Fifteen more minutes and he'll have to head back. He hates the thought of it. Way up ahead, he sees a municipal building with long windows. Two flags in front of it, slowly dropping from a pole, flare out suddenly in a flash of wind. It's something big and bright he's feeling. Warm on the outside, cool on the inside. He doesn't know a soul here, he's sure of it. Hardly knows he's walking, so buoyed up by the clear air, the sun-drenched street.

But time is passing, just the same.

The "now loading" call carries halfway down the block. Val bursts through the doors of the waiting room—not a minute too soon. The familiar crowd is massing at the side of the bus. "Thought we'd lost you," Old Pastels waves. Soon as he sees him, Val turns on his heels. He's not getting back on. No way. Better have his suitcase pulled right now.

But that's sooner decided than done; it's all very leisurely in the baggage department, where the handler sits tipped back on a slanting chair, his shoes propped up on the counter. A most delicate balance. "I'm in a hurry," says Val, holding out his claim ticket. The handler reaches for it in slow motion, gives it the long arm treatment. "Cal-i-forn-ey"–he reads, squinting–"land of fruit and nuts."

"I'm in a hurry."

"Who isn't? So you come in at the last minute? You had plenty of time–how long a layover?"

"Changed my mind," is all Val owes him by way of explanation. "It's a free country," he throws in. It's nobody's business where he gets on and off. "Will you hurry?"

The handler clatters down to ground level. "What color you say that was?"

Color? He must choose. "Brown," he guesses. The word clots in his throat. Most suitcases are brown, aren't they? What if he's mistaken?

The bus is still fuming at the loading dock, but the last boarding call has gone out.

Val doesn't look back. He can hear the bus behind him, swinging out of the station.

He's relieved to have his suitcase, but walking with a load is different–not so fine and free. Same shops and parking lots, though the light has altered, the angle shifted. In the doorway of a bridal shop, Val is startled to see another human figure. That's what it is, though so stooped over himself he might be mistaken for a sack of something. "How's your mother?" he calls out anxiously. It might be to Val, it might be to the air; there are no other options. Val says nothing. "Nice weather," the voice continues. Val says nothing to this, either.

Already the streetlights are coming on. There's a whiff of cattle on the wind; must be a feedlot nearby. Val puts down his suitcase and rests under a sign that says PRAISALS. A pawnshop, but there's only a twist of jumper cables, a sack of livestock feed, and a three-colored cat drowsing in the window. The wind's freshening—what now? The streets branching out to the left from here are dark, the pavement broken. Off to the right, it looks brighter. In fact, this probably isn't the main street, but it's all he knows; he can trust it to lead him back to the bus terminal if nothing pans out. What he'll do is go straight on to the next traffic light and make a decision when he gets there.

REVCO DRUGS . . . CHRISTIAN OFFICE SUPPLY . . . HIS PLACE (Christian Books) . . . Restaurant ahead—just beyond the traffic light. That will be his first stop. But when he gets close he finds that it, too, is shut tight. The sign in the window says OPEN, but the chairs are stacked upside down on the tables and the lights are out. He rattles the doorknob: useless, then spots the smaller notice dangling below the knob:

SORRY, WE'RE CLOSED

So now what? The handle of his suitcase is biting into his palm; he's famished; he'll settle for anything. If he doesn't find something soon, might as well turn around and board the next bus out.

Last try.

Lights beckon up ahead, where the road bends. He'll go that way.

Coming near, he's disappointed to learn that the building the lights are coming from is the public library. Still, the place looks cozy. He's chilled through and through, and sick of hauling his suitcase around. He needs to put down his load, to sit and think a while before moving on. Suitcase must look queer, but here goes—fast—

Safely through, he stands a minute to take his bearings. Something not quite right here . . . The NO SPITTING —NO STARING sign, for one thing. And what else? If you're busy at the catalog or the shelves, you might not catch on.

At first glance they might pass for readers, but not on second. They've taken over the browsing chairs. One's sleeping, a John Deere cap pulled down low over his eyes; another's just sitting, arms folded, eyes glassy, zonked out for sure. A boy in overalls is turning over the pages of *Fortune* magazine, daintily, his fingernails ragged, black with grime.

Val heads for the long bench; it's less comfortable looking than the chairs but there's only the one man sitting there, so plenty of room to spare. Busy stuffing his gums with chewing tobacco, he doesn't bother to look up when Val settles alongside. Val plants his suitcase between his feet. "Traveling?" the man inquires.

"I'm here now," Val says.

"This closes up pretty soon—half an hour, I think. Got a place for the night?"

Bad news for Val. His face must show it, because the man says, "Stay with us," and he tells Val about the Everlasting Arms around the corner. Supper, breakfast, bed for the night, no questions asked. Most of those sitting here are going over that way, they're killing time till chapel. You go to chapel or you don't eat–that's the deal.

The Everlasting Arms is built like an army barracks–unpainted aluminum siding, rippled iron roof. There's a billboard giving advance warning half a block ahead:

IF YOU ARE HUNGRY, DO NOT BEG OR STEAL

COME EAT WITH US

Val is hungry, hollow with it. The man he's with introduces himself as Jack. Val doesn't feel ready to give over his name; he calls himself "Vince." Jack doesn't offer his last name, so Val's under no obligation there.

Jack spits his plug at the last minute, at the very portals of the Everlasting Arms. He leads Val to a desk, where Val, reluctantly, hands in his suitcase. "It'll be safe," Jack assures him, "that's why they do it. If you don't lock it up, chain it or nail it to the ground, don't count on finding it in the morning."

Val wants to know: "You believe any of this?", but they're swinging through the chapel doors, they're inside now, in a hush, and he never gets around to asking. Now that he no longer has the suitcase grounding him, Val's unsure of his footing. Or maybe the floor's overwaxed, maybe that's the point–to give a down-the-slippery-slope feeling. Jack's striding on ahead to a pew that's front and center. The red runner down the center aisle looks like it might give more traction, but it's too public. Val has no intention of going that route.

The Black Suit waiting on the platform up front has got to be the preacher. Skinhead, wouldn't you know it, a few poor gray hairs trussed up over his naked scalp to give him some cover. Silver specs, the works.

A piano piping in from someplace, high up. The music must be canned; there's no piano on the premises as far as Val can see. He stares down at his shoes during the opening prayer. If this is what you have to do for a free feed, he'll do it. Whatever it takes. The preacher says, "We rise for the reading of God's word." Val stands.

"May God add his blessing to the reading of his word."

God's word for today is Ezekiel, something about digging a hole in the wall and spying out abominations: "Hast thou seen what the ancients of the house of Israel do in the dark, every man in the chambers of his imagery? For they say, 'The Lord seeth us not; the Lord hath forsaken the earth.'" The preacher lifts his hands, then lets them flap, settle, like he's bringing down a piano cover. They sit.

Somebody coughs, and a round of coughing begins.

Sitting, rising, the stiff rows of chairs, put Val in mind of a room like this. Where? It's a blank, mostly. A few things he can recall, though. He was up front, his hand on the rail, a dark, gleaming wood rail, he remembers the cool, smooth feel of it. What else? The rows back of him were empty. Not like here.

Everyone up front shouting when he walked out . . .

"For they say, 'The Lord seeth us not; the Lord hath forsaken the earth.' When the wind blows, the dirt flies . . . When you're as depressed, as blown away as a norther in West Texas, remember this: God sees. He doesn't blink and He doesn't miss a thing. God knows how many hairs you have on your head. Believe it! He's got an eye for fine detail. I lost four hairs combing this morning; God pointed his little finger and subtracted them. Better not be subtracted! Better take a good look at yourselves now. God doesn't make tramps. That's not my opinion— it's the opinion of the word of God. Did you know that money is spoken of over seven hundred times in the Bible? And that's only direct mention; indirectly, it's many, many times more. Money is important to God. Yessir! You betcha! It's the will of God for his people to have nice homes."

I had a nice home, Val reminds himself. Worked for years to pay for that apartment and fix it up nice. To build up a collection—

I loved what I bought.

"God's not a bum." The preacher's still harping on it. "How many of you believe that if God came in off the street He'd be dirty?"

A hand in one of the side pews goes up. Then down quick, seeing it's alone.

Val yawns until his jaws crack; it's all he can do to keep his head propped up, eyes open. His hunger is played out now, sleep gaining on him, everything slow, sludged with sleep. The preacher's still at it. "God . . . God . . . God," the word like a bite or a yawn bitten back . . . and Val's inside somewhere some chamber of imagery bleared grass flowing by like water green water the slither of lights in black water, he's sliding, he's—

hurled—

"God don't sponsor no flops! It's the devil that delights in failure."

Val, jolted awake, sees the men in front of him riding

in rows, shuffling and coughing in rows. They look crouched and small, and a smell of uncleanness is upon them.

"You didn't walk in here by accident," the preacher struts. "You walked in by divine decree, by divine ordination." Somebody murmurs "Ah-men!" to that, stretching the sound–some fink, no doubt hired for the purpose. May it stick in his throat, Val prays, may they all choke on it, for now every last one of them is chiming in.

The story next, there's always a story. This is a long one about a man who buys a house but lets somebody else buy a nail in the wall of the house. Couple of mornings after he moves in, he finds a dead dog hanging from that nail, so, naturally, he wants to pull out the whole mess. And that's the one thing he can't do, because the nail doesn't belong to him. That nail is the devil's stake in the property, and when the dog begins to stink to high heaven, the man is forced to sell the house.

"Never a sin too small . . ." Val studies the sun-creased neck and bowed head of the man in front of him. Dog . . . house . . . nail . . . The story's a chamber of imagery, but what does it mean? Where's the drift?

Preacher is coming to that. The drift–the point of it all–is sin. "Sin–that one small breach in the wall that the devil stakes out. What good does it do to own the house when the devil owns the nail?

"Pick a sin, any sin will do. There are no small sins. All sin is serious. Sin is disobedience and rebellion against God and always, always, self-destruction. Death is my shepherd . . . Marijuana is my green pasture . . . Whiskey is the water of my soul . . ."

Val presses his knuckles against the back of the pew. Harder. Something about prairie fires now. Only where the fire has been can we be safe. Only where the wrath of God has already been. That's me, thinks Val. That's Calvary, says the preacher.

"Let us go to the Lord in prayer." They are winding down.

Val lifts the songbook from the pew rack and fans through it, hunting for the hymn of invitation. The others must be old hands at this, for no one else is bothering with the book. And they're singing with conviction now, "Just as I am without one plea," singing for their suppers, their throats lifted.

Just as they are, they file into the dining hall. Three lines of ten and a few stragglers, they inch forward in silence. Cardboard plates, plastic forks and knives. Val recognizes Jack in a soiled white apron, standing behind the counter, coils of steam rising around him. He waves a long spoon at Val. Hired help, as Val suspected all along. Some kind of scout.

Sloppy joe, mashed potato, black-eyed peas, pie on the side—it's not first-class but it's filling. They bend over their trays, prayerlike, deep and quiet now. The old man next to Val is the first to finish. He sits, shredding a Styrofoam cup with his teeth, staring off at a point on the wall, a circle of new paint on the faded yellow. Something round, a clock, must have hung there. Val checks his own watch: they've still a stretch till bedtime.

After "Rec Hour"—a little Ping-Pong, a lot of standing and staring—they line up to take a leak. The man behind him taps Val on the shoulder and introduces him-

self as Jerry. Has something he wants to share. "Oh, no thanks," says Val.

"No trouble. Hold your water," Jerry smiles. There's white, something milky, at the corners of his lips. "Ready now?" He's holding a deck of cards in his hand. Card tricks, Val thinks; but, no, he's handing them over. Box says LES GIRLES. Val opens the box and flips through a few to get the man off his back.

No news here: it's a stack of girls with nothing on, or only a little something, sequins or feathers, to spice it up. There's a girl spilling out of a bathrobe; girl with the ghost of a bathing suit, a two-tone tan; a girl in heat, back arched, thrashing around in a bathtub full of Wheaties–good wholesome fun is the idea. Little come-on underneath each picture: DIANA DESIRES. She's four of hearts. NOTHING TO DO? I'M CANDY. DO IT WITH ME. Two of diamonds. A girl in high boots, black leather belt with a big brass buckle, and not a blessed other thing on her but skin. Fake leopard couch in the background. Whip in hand? No. Innocent pleasures, these. IF YOU ARE A FETISH MAN YOU WILL LOVE MY FANTASY LAND. WANDA. Seven of hearts.

"Such shit," says Val, stuffing them back in the box.

"Wait a minute–you missed the best." Jerry reaches for the deck and shuffles it with an expert hand. "Huh? How's this? Name's Ting Ling." It's a Chink, skinny, not a stitch, sitting in a wicker chair, bunch of roses in her hand. Ace of hearts. TING LING FOR YOU. I'll bet, thinks Val. Dots her "i's" with little itsy bitsy hearts; he knows her type.

"So dumb," says Val. "I've seen them all before."

"Can't be the same," says Jerry. "These are the new ones, they're just out."

They line up again for beds, turning over their valuables to a man with a clipboard who makes them sign for them. Val can't remember what name he called himself to Jack–was it Vic? Vince?–so he puts down only the initial "V." He turned over his suitcase when he first came through the door, and all he has left is wallet, watch and keys–the keys useless from here on out. He gives over everything but his watch; he'll take the risk; it's all that ties him into the world right now. The man with the clipboard hands him a plastic disk with a number: eight.

Stashing the eight in his pocket, he comes up with an old lottery ticket, the combination blocked in with heavy pencil strokes: one, two, three–not very original but, someday, by the law of averages, he was bound to score. What goes round comes round, so they say.

The door of the dormitory cuffs him as it swings open. It hits him then: the eye-watering sting of disinfectant, the cots in hospital rows, the painted Jesus, big, bigger than life-size, sprawled across the wall. He's never seen a Jesus this blond or this comfortable; he might be just lounging on the cross and saying, "No sweat, no hassle."

Val finds the bed with the number eight marked on the topsheet, peels down to his shorts, tucks his shoes under the mattress, and stretches out. Maybe in the morning he'll take a shower, but first things first.

Right now, he's whipped. Tight as a fist. Too tense to sleep, so he stares at the spotted ceiling, trying to unclench. The voices come at him. Someone, just over his head:

Would you answer the question yes or no?

And his own voice:

I'm going to tell you. It answers your question. It answers your question. Will you listen?

And the answer, mocking:

Very carefully.

When he wakes next, nearly all the beds are occupied. There's a desk in the middle of the room, a white-haired man sitting there, glancing up from his reading now and then to watch them.

Val studies the watchman through half-closed lids. The others are dim capsules around him. The room is noisy with the muffled sounds of digestion, somebody somewhere coughing, somebody sawing logs, this soft, broken buzz. Upstairs or far away, a phone is ringing. Nobody answering, but it keeps right on. A thin sound, like a thin cold ray. Val sees in its pitiless light all he has lost: his car, his beautiful things, his job, his girl, his good name. His memory.

When was it he'd started out? Could it be only days ago? By now it seems another country, another life, so far away, this long limbo of motion in between. He strains to retrieve landmarks, recalls a sign, can see the green oblong in his mind's eye, the white letters of THIRD AVENUE bright and clear, in perfect focus, but cannot quite see the sign attached at right angles to that, the number of the street, it's just out of sight . . . He strains so hard to see it that water comes out of his eyes.

One other thing: a drugstore, he used to stare at it from his bedroom window, its sign a mortar and pestle in moving lights. The lights were stalled. He spent hours staring at that sign, not knowing what he saw, standing at the window, waiting for his girl to come home. And feeling–what? No feeling. That's entirely blanked out. He had a serious job, but cannot, for the life of him, recall what it was. He was good at his job, whatever it was, he'd plugged away at it, planned ahead. Was it sales? Certain words . . . "price angle" . . . "low-end merchandise" come to mind, the "four 'P's' "–a formula: "product, price, placement, publicity," then the silver stud, a service pin he'd worn in his lapel, there were two linked letters–a company insignia of some kind. His tongue scrapes his palate seeking a clue to the letters, the name, a fragment of sound. Only a dry clapping, word of emptiness. Years of service down the drain. He's so beat.

He sleeps again, wakes again.

Two in the morning. The man at the desk is dozing, slumped over his book. Everyone sleeping, folded into their dreams. *The Lord has fled.* A truck shifts gears, passes. Somebody moans in his sleep, sounds like a lamb bleating. *The Lord has fled the earth.* How far? How long ago?

The warmth of day has fled. Val is free. There is no place on earth where he is tied. No one on earth has a hook on him. Nobody. Tomorrow he'll be starting over.

He sleeps again, wakes again. He checks his wrist. Still here, still clicking. Six: zero four: never mind the seconds. He's here: among the living, still in the ruts of time.

Henrietta's Morning

"It's six oh five in the morning . . ."

No light in the body yet.

There's static in the background, sounds like eggs frying. Then silence. Then clear speaking. Henrietta cracks one gritted eye open to the radiant dial.

What a joy it is, what a joy, he says, to be part of the morning world where wings legs voices, the milo and the triticale, the wheat and, yes, the Johnson grass are stirring. Even the Johnson grass!—the tares with the wheat. Brother Ames is all apraise, all ajoying. And how is God's creature yourself this fine and early morning?

None too swift.

She waits for weather, but Brother Ames is too busy praising the weeds to get round to it. She'll have to see for herself. Thumbing back the shade, she peers up the long street.

Scorcher, another one.

Not yet out of bed and already she's feeling poky. Henrietta doesn't know whether it's the unseasonable early heat or her bad teeth causing it. She'd like to rest till she figures it out, but resting's out of the question.

"On that day, the fox shall nest in a turnip—"

Hasten the day!

"And the wheat shall be harvested on the day it is sown."

One of these days . . . it's coming soon. Been counting on it for so long.

But—plant and harvest on the very same day? Must mean time is closing down. That's a hard thought—impossible, really, to get the hang of. Henrietta stares blankly at the row of doll faces on the dresser. "Morning, gals," she greets them. They smile back like they always do, morning, noon and night.

"And each grain of wheat shall weigh the same as the kidney of an ox."

Now that's stretching it.

"And the fruit trees shall bear fruit the day they are planted. And not only the fruit be sweet, but also the bark and the wood!" Brother Ames is really flowering things up. Give us a normal wheat harvest in due course, she thinks, or the whole of Jayroe County will dry up and blow away.

"And not only the fruit trees—all trees shall bear

fruit. They that sow in tears shall reap in joy. When the Lord reigns and judgment's done . . ."

She can hear Brother Ames going on, just the hum of it—not the particular words—as she flings on her kimono and makes her way down the hall. In the bathroom mirror, she catches only a family likeness to who she once was. How did the line of her eyebrows go, the true line? No telling now. And better not search too long: it's near hopeless. Left one needs a tweeze, that's all she knows; she feathers it up, then smooths it. Still don't match: right one's loopier, higher.

Hopeless! Looks like somebody put a print of her face on a dish towel and wrung it out. She'd been a real good-looker once. Been Miss Wayside of 1947, Miss Rattlesnake Queen of 1948, and only missed being Miss Wheatheart of Jayroe and Letsem Counties by breaking her ankle the day before. So May Musick got the crown instead.

And look at May now! Three chins and married to Tom Stowe, who is nothing to brag on.

Those summers, it seemed like Henrietta was always smiling. But it wasn't only the summers—even the darkest winters were shining. They didn't have a whole lot—nothing special—but what they had seemed magic. On winter nights, those bitter long nights, there were sparkle parties. A bunch of them would gather at Angie's house; at the signal "lights out," they'd start popping wintergreen Life Savers, grinding them with their teeth till the sweet splinters prickled and sparked. If you opened your mouth then and squinched your eyes, you could see a spray of sparks, sea green, flashing. Sam Plemons and she once went into a closet to do it. They don't make Life Savers that way anymore.

Those were the days, a joy to awaken.

While nowadays–Henrietta can't hardly bear to face herself until she gets her foundation applied and her lashes glued on. She lifts one lash from its platform, flexes it, then does the same thing with the other–they're still new. With a toothpick, she dabs adhesive along the edge of the lash strip. Caref–how those little suckers do stick! Eye shadow (pearly blue today), blusher (honey rose), lipstick (Moulin Rouge). There we go. Hair a little too poofy in front? Just tamp it. Easy– That'll do it.

"If you need a church home"–Brother Ames is signing off–"soul's rest, a burden lifted . . ." Henrietta has a church home, but the burden's not lifting. The Lord, she figures, is dealing with her heart.

Something's going to come out of all her grieving, all her losing. Something, somebody, sometime. She smooths the pink bedspread, plumping the magenta and black velvet pillows that dress it up to look like a couch. Two by two, she carries her dolls over from the dresser and lounges them against the pillows. She has four girls: Terri, Kianne, Lucy and Kate. Kate's the floppy one, stuffed with rags, her smiling head always lolling on her chest.

These days, Henrietta seems to be always waiting. Nights, she rattles around the apartment like one big pea in a pod. There are times, small hours of the night, when she'll reach for the phone and dial the weather to hear a voice, any human voice. And there are times when she

goes clear beyond feeling, beyond tears even. Those are the worst times of all.

At least Henrietta knows she is saved, that's the main thing. Of course, she's been saved before. The first time she walked down the aisle and gave her heart to Jesus she was fourteen. That didn't last long. Soon enough, she was backslidden, busy having a good time though sick with sin, till thirty-two and the divorce from Joe. Backslidden again in her middle thirties when Charlie came along and she was saved again. Lost again when Charlie died. Saved again at fifty-two. Still slippery at fifty-seven, still struggling, though her feet are on the rock and, with the Lord's help, she will persevere.

By the time she turns down Travis Street, her feet are sweating. Travis–Bowie–Crockett–nearly there. The lawn in Long Stretch Cemetery looks hairy and hot. That's where Charlie is now, the baby beside him. You can't make them out from here, they're farther back, over the rise. Charlie's says SEE YOU LATER, he was always saying that. The other says OUR SWEET, and the date, the one day she came and went.

REST EASY . . . It's like reading an autograph album, walking along the fence, passing the LOVED BY ALL, the GONE BUT NOT FORGOTTEN, the TOGETHER FOREVER. Then, in a smaller hand: PRECIOUS (shaped like a valentine), GOD'S GIFT FOR A WHILE, ANGEL, GOD ALONE UNDERSTANDS. When she comes to the granite basketball on a pillar, the stone that says TAKE ME HOME, she crosses the street.

And there it is: Henrietta's restaurant.

She named it Three Square Meals when she started ten years back, but most people called it "Henrietta's

Cemetery Restaurant," because the cemetery was so close and so many of her customers were people coming in from a burying or an unveiling. They'd drop in for a pick-me-up before going back into their lives.

The place is always musty this time of morning. First thing she has to do is open all the windows in the kitchen and prop open the door to the alley to let the morning pour through. Better start up the fans now, before Stella gets the stove going.

Next, she tends to the message board. The special for today is chicken, hot biscuits and cream gravy. She writes GOLDEN BROWN CHICKEN to brighten it up. The breakfast menu stays as is: SHORT STACK, STACK, TWO-BY-FOUR (two eggs with four small pancakes), EGGS, EGGS WITH HASBROWNS (make that HASH) and COMBOS.

Nothing to do now but get the coffee started. Once that's done, she sets herself down at the table nearest the cash register and takes stock. It would be fair to say, as Ida Looper did, that Henrietta is "house proud." She enjoys the fruits of her labors. Goodness yes, isn't she entitled? She glances up at her trophies, from the lucky first dollar in cellophane over the cash register to the three knives crossed like the staves of a wigwam, framed against velvet, on the wall with the pie safe.

The knives come from the course she took at the A-1 Cooking School in Letsem City. Henrietta had been the best, and at the end of the semester they'd given her the three knives as a prize: the all-purpose chef's knife, the little tiny three-inch paring knife, and the long narrow boning knife. She'd been first prizewinner at deboning a Cornish game hen. Click, click, click, all the little bones whisked away and none the worse for wear. It took her quite a number of birds before she was able to do it so the little thing lay there–not like a puddle, but still starched and standing–with its fine peaked chest shaped as the good Lord shaped it.

"Morning!" The back door bangs. Stella's in.

"Morning," Henrietta calls back. How the live voice livens things!

Something is going to happen today, Henrietta is sure of it. Somebody coming, walking into her life. If not today, then tomorrow. Soon. She can tell.

Henrietta prides herself on her gift of discernment. She never even knew what it was or that she had it until that time at revival when Sister Ora Burch stared at Henrietta, tapped her own forehead, and said, "Henrietta, I believe you've got the gift of discernment." And it was true: Henrietta could see things she couldn't say, could see with a man like Oral Roberts how his eyes weren't on God. And with her landlady, the one back on Line Street, who pretended to be a good Christian lady, Henrietta knew, just knew, she had demons, for she could see another pair of eyes, icy-gray, peeping out through her landlady's eyes. And after she spied out those double eyes, the landlady would run away whenever she saw Henrietta coming.

That was how Henrietta knew she had the gift of discernment.

Ordinary Time

Anarrow night, but it is over. He's been thrashing for hours. He cannot remember what he dreamed, except for the sound of sweeping, somebody sweeping the floor in darkness. Must have been the wind.

Five after six. The hands of the clock are faint wavering lines; the book, the cup alongside, mere smudges.

The curtain breathes. The shade slowly whitens, slaps against the sill.

Only the crucifix on the wall is becalmed: the shape of a bird, he thinks, with outstretched wings. A bird of prey, hovering. Waiting.

Raising himself on one elbow, Father Gilvary leans

over and lifts the shade. Cranks up his waking prayer, "Lord, open my lips, and let," when something shimmers: a flowering shrub, caught in the wind, bending brightly like a fountain.

It occurs to him that the lawn badly needs a mowing.

Father Gilvary repeats, "Lord, open my lips," and this time says it straight through to the end. Yawns. Clears his throat: coughs a gob of phlegm into his water cup. That's better.

"Good morning?"

Nothing answers. The shades on the facing houses are still drawn.

Then, directly across from him, in perfect silence, a flock of birds breaks out of a tree as if the tree itself is breaking, particles of tree rising–

"Good morning!"

And there, on the rectory fence, something flickers– a sparrow, settling.

"Where've you been?"

The sparrow comes closer, to the very edge of the sill. They are eye to eye. The quick, glittering eye is questioner. The other, slow, steady, dim, gives no answer. Its dark center deepens, though.

Eyes hold for a moment. "We are alive in this together," Father Gilvary whispers. Only a moment–then a blur of motion and the fence stands. Bare as it's ever been.

It is time–time to be up and about. Ordinary time, Father Gilvary reminds himself, the longest, and hardest, season of the liturgical year. But, why hard? When the message–*the reign of God is already in your midst*–is so simple . . . Not in the mighty wind, nor in the earth-

quake, nor in the blazing fire, but in the murmuring
breeze, the still, small voice. In the yeast working unseen
through three measures of flour. In Jesus and Peter paying
the temple tax, half a shekel each; Paul instructing the
Thessalonians, no goldbricking while waiting around for
the apocalypse: *continue quietly working and earning the
food you eat.*

Be here now.

What could be easier than this?

Almost anything, actually . . . Great occasions:
miracles, rescues, tribulations, scourges. Epic sacrifice.
Anything sudden and vivid with trumpets blazing on high.
Anything—anything but the long laboring for the kingdom, the following-through, the daily round, *adding goodness to faith, understanding to goodness, patience to understanding,* and something more—is it devotion?—to patience,
kindness to devotion . . . ? He cannot recall all the links
in the chain, but he remembers the last, the clincher: *and
to this kindness, love.* From Second Peter, in the readings
coming up. Self-control tossed in there somewhere, too.
Not at all simple, no. Not easy. He touches the wall as he
moves down the corridor. Firm. He touches the doorpost.
He touches the smooth rim of the sink, the silk of the
mirror. All familiar. After the valleys and peaks of Lent,
and Triduum, the flights of Easter and Pentecost, they are
back to the flatlands of time, to the time between the
Times.

Absently, Father Gilvary runs his toothbrush over
his eyebrows which are shaggy from sleep. Next, he applies paste and puts the brush to proper use. Sour mouth,
the scum of bad sleep, he can taste it. He rinses. Still there.

His teeth look mossy, grayish—that's age—beyond remedy. There's a smudge on the mirror. He swipes at it with two fingers, then with a damp washrag. Still there. The silver behind the glass must be tarnished; it's an old mirror, after all. He sighs, lathering up his long cheeks, and shaves thoughtfully. Then doles out a capful of green mouth-wash. His gargle is an inflexible morning ritual; he looks forward to it, shocking his sinuses clean, needling his mouth awake. The sound of his gagging is terrible, tuber-cular, but there is no one around to hear it.

Opening the church doors, Father Gilvary feels how hot and dry it is. Already. The wind has a harsh, sandpapery feel. For weeks they've been waiting for rain: the wheat is parched. He has a prayer for rain written out somewhere. Question is where. In the old Sacramentary?

Green vestments today. It is ordinary time.

Shortly before seven, two elderly women enter the church. "I never liked her," says the first, dabbing the holy water in the font and stroking from forehead to collar-bone; then, signing from left shoulder to right, adds fer-vently, "and I never shall."

At ten of seven, Father Gilvary vests in the sacristy, mouthing soundlessly the words that have become part of his private ritual of preparation, *for the partaking of this bread, which I, all unworthy, make bold to receive,* praying not to become a castaway, to forever cling. At five of seven, he prods Michael, the acolyte, to his feet. At seven, he enters the sanctuary. He bows, kisses the altar, sketches a cross in air. The faithful number eight this morning: Genevieve, Sue, Marge, the Bremen sisters (his Mary and Martha), Rosie, Ronda, and Nova.

"The Lord be with you."

"And also with you."

An ordinary Mass in ordinary time. Yet never ordinary as he lifts his hands over the altar, or leans over the circle of bread.

"He broke the bread . . ." Father Gilvary raises the host, shakily, too high. "Take this, all of you, and eat it," his fingers tightly pressed.

And Michael, stirring from his torpor, lifts the bells. They make a trailing sound from the elevation all the way down.

How many times, and with what patience, has Father Gilvary explained to Michael that the bell is not there for decoration? That the bell comes at the instant of elevation, only at the peak, at the proclamation, "Do this in memory of Me," that it signifies: "Behold it!—behold the miraculous transubstantiation now accomplished, bread into Body, wine into Blood." And Michael blinks, nods to show that he's heard, but the point is never grasped. It would be useless going through the lecture again.

"When supper was ended he took the cup." Light streams from the Saint Jude window.

"Take this, all of you, and drink from it." His thumb flattens on the ridged circle at the base of the chalice where his mother's wedding ring is hammered in. *You have given us wine to drink that makes us reel.* He holds the chalice high, at an alarming angle. Rose light spills through his fingers.

"This is the cup of my blood—"

Meat

The animal tumbles through the trapdoor, head first, down the chute. Sometimes the body is still twitching when the hook goes in. He knows that the animal, plugged between the eyes, does not feel. Nor does he, Val, feel anything. He is part of the machine. He wears ear stoppers, a white hard hat, and a white lab coat. His arm cuts a shining path through the air. Five times a minute, the trapdoor opens, the animal falls. The animals, hooked by one leg, rumble past him on chains. Five a minute.

Val's first job in Durance is at GPMP–the Great Plains Meat Packing Company. His job is to make the first rump cut. From it will come round steak, pot roast, eye of round and heel of round.

It is time and motion: he must make five strokes a minute. His arm comes out at the root to strike at the rump. His arm comes back out of the rump. Five times a minute. He watches the knife, the arm–his arm–move. Knife and arm are one. They move apart from him. They are part of the machine. If he misses the rhythm, he, too, will become meat, cut down by the machine.

His thumb aches.

There's a rhythm, like question and answer. *You don't remember?* Now stroke and now lift. *I loved what I bought.* Arm and rump, arm and– *The hammer you don't?* If he loses the count–*Will you let me explain?*–he loses the job. *I'm waiting to hear.* His fingers are cramped. *My wife just walked out*–the the small fingers numb–

She wasn't your wife.

His ears are stoppered, the air is fogged. The tongues of the meat hang down. They film the employees, the time-and-motion men, hunting for eyes that shift, for eyes that dream. They show him how the hand must hold: contact grasp; punch grasp; wrap grasp. Val must look at the rump only, straight ahead. The floor is slippery with blood and with floating gobbets of fat. He wears galoshes standing in blood.

It's a procession. Up the line, the legs are spread. Saws divide the rib cage; the chest is emptied into a heaping cart. The heap glistens and slides, and steam goes up from it. The air is cold.

The choice cuts, the lesser cuts, are taken, the knives know where to go. It's like spreading seams. The knives know how. Knives, curved and pronged, pointed and forked, sing in the air.

The knives are prime. A young Vietnamese wraps his up in a T-shirt, goes home and stabs his girlfriend and himself. It is all over the newspaper, front page, but nobody at GPMP mentions it. Everybody has knives, saws or air guns, and blood is slippery underfoot.

Nobody talks much on the job.

Val lasts all of a week. The money is good, but that's it. One paycheck gets him out of the Everlasting Arms, though, and into a rooming house where he can come and go as he pleases. And no more chapel. The house is yellow with a slat fence strung along all sides of it, a long porch and a sign in front that says PRIVACY RESPECTED and CASH ONLY.

It's full of old ladies that keep to themselves. Val can hear them bolting their chains whenever he passes down the hall at night. Fine with him.

He buys a radio, an enamel pot for the hot plate that comes with the room, paper plates, a glass bowl, and some plastic eating utensils—the kind for picnics. He still has some cash to spare, but he doesn't know when his next job will come or what it will be. He's not going back into sales if he can help it. He thinks he might be able to do warehouse inventory or yard work, or maybe even learn forklifting—that shouldn't be too strenuous, some kind of job where he puts in his hours and when he leaves he's quit of it. He reads the want ads. There's plenty of yard work but weed pulling doesn't pay beans, and he hasn't got the muscle for truck loading, sandblasting or irrigation pit cleaning. Anybody can tell at a glance that he's been a desk man, city slick.

He's got to have a job. Out of work, he spends hours doodling in his mind. He'll do anything to drown out the voices—one question, over and over: *So we'll leave that in the air?* He marks up the want ads, then phones; like they say, it beats walking. But even by phone he wastes a lot of time. It wears him down, holding the "hold line," listening to all that so-sorry-be-with-you-in-a-minute music. And, sometimes, after all that waiting, he gets the wrong department and it's back to Musicland.

He walks the streets of Durance, wondering why he stays. The town is bigger, more spread out than he thought, but there is nothing to see here. Nothing going on. People drive to their jobs downtown and drive home. Evenings, they sit on their porches and watch the sprinklers whirl; it's an event, a regular light show.

What he likes is all the space. The slack. The spaces between houses here. Spaces where streets lose themselves in prairie. Spaces between people, nobody pushing into his space, nothing boxing him in. Everything loose and far apart.

Only thing is: he's got to have a job. He sits in the park, double-checking the want ads in case he's missed anything. He hasn't.

He's got to find a job, yes, but just a minute, that sun is so— Won't be mild for long. He leans back, basking, with half-closed eyes.

Then he spies something on the rim of sight—somebody standing and watching. A kid, tall and gawky, with that dead-white skin that only redheads have. Eyeglasses.

Meat

Val watches him move along the perimeter of the park, making the rounds of the wire baskets. Fishing for bottles and cans, looks like, dragging a sack after him.

And heading this way. Val mimes sleep, shutting his eyes fast, but he can feel the shadow fall, something blocking his light. When he opens his eyes he knows what he'll find.

The kid says "Hi," nothing more. Shoots this teeny tiny scrap of paper into Val's hand with a sidearm motion and moves on by.

There's not much to it:

INVITE HIM

INTO YOUR HEART

Must be an ad for a church of some kind, but the name isn't given, only a post office box number.

Time for Val to hustle. The scrap of paper is sticking to his fingers; he flicks it off. It's getting to Val—all this holy stuff. He's picking it up everywhere in Durance, over the radio, on billboards and walls. Even the traffic signs are scribbled over: YIELD—TO JESUS, STOP—SIN. And the urinals are full of it, along with the usual four-letter words, and something sicko about using niggers for mud flaps.

But here's Travis Street, new to him.

FONG'S GOLDEN SKILLET . . . TOYOTA . . . TRUE VALUE HARDWARE . . . GOD'S LITTLE HOT DOG STAND (Christian groceries) . . . AEROMOTOR WINDMILL WORKS. He turns left on Bowie, down Fanin.

Nothing doing here. The heat's really stoking up.

He'll try one more—it's Crockett—treeless, a street scratched with sunlight. DURANCE MONUMENT COMPANY, BLUE SKY DENIMS, MEMORAIL—he looks twice to make sure—FLOWERS.

Fairway ahead. No, look again, it's a boneyard. Called LONG STRETCH—that's rich . . . Up ahead, other side of the street, there's a big house with the shades drawn and a sign: FATHER & SON. Very mysterious. He's about to call it a day, another lost day, when he catches sight of an eating place across from the cemetery. He's parched. A tall glass of water with ice making a sweat on it would be heaven. And to sit under a moving fan.

It's called THREE SQUARE MEALS. A bright orange notice is taped to the door:

FULL MEAL DEAL

BEST MEAL IN TOWN

COME QUINCH YOUR THIRST

There's a menu posted and, under it, a HELP WANTED sign. Can't be much of a job, but what does he have to lose?

It's a wait and see.

The place is mostly open tables, but there are two tall booths in back, both unoccupied. Val makes his way to the second booth, even though the table's still cluttered with dishes. The big blonde at the cash register hollers for somebody to come out and clear, and a brown girl comes out of the kitchen, carrying a tray and a rag. Then the blonde gathers up a menu and a pitcher of ice water and heads toward him.

She's quite a sight, the blond one. All lit up. Looks like one of those painting-by-the-numbers jobs. Gumdrop colors: bright yellow hair, pink cheeks, red lips, green eyelids. Lashes like scrub brushes.

Standing and staring at him like she just might read his mind. All he really wants is water, but if he intends to sit a while he'd better order something. So he asks for coffee and pie.

They have pecan, apple and cherry.

"Any kind of pie," he says.

Then he leans back in the booth and listens. Conversation spills over the tables. First names–place seems to be full of regulars. An old man in overalls shuffles in. "How you doing, George?" The blonde at the register starts it, and a chorus takes it up.

"Better than nothing," George says.

Val wishes he could say as much. He can't say he's better than nothing–or worse than nothing–or different from nothing.

Trick or treat–before he knows it, the blonde is back. She points to his cup: "Liven that up for you?"

"Guess not," he says.

"It's for free. First refills are on the house."

So he puts out his cup. "Say when," she says. He doesn't, and she fills it. Now's as good a time as any–

"Saw the sign," he begins.

"It was a waitress, a girl, I had in mind," she says.

"Oh, well then."

"But we might could use a man," she adds. "Ever waited on tables? Done any kitchen work?"

"No," he says, "and I never worked for women's wages, either."

He can tell she's sizing him up. "Extra wages for extra work," she says. "We could use a man."

He's not jumping.

"If you're serious about working, why don't you get

on back to the kitchen and help Stella stack the dishes. She'd be glad of some help. If you're serious."

"I am serious," he says.

"Well, don't set and think too long or I'll give the job to somebody else. There's plenty be glad of the chance."

Val puts his hand up. "Wait a sec–I need to digest."

"Not much time for that here. Not for the help anyway." He's done with his pie, so she takes his plate. "You near ready?"

He takes a long swallow of water, makes a face. "Why does it taste so funny?"

" 'Gyppy,' we call it. Got gypsum in it, some days more than others. Look, if you want the job–fine, if you don't–fine."

Val rouses himself. She leads him to the swing doors of the kitchen. Hand on the door, she turns and asks, "Whereabouts are you from?"

"Ohio."

"Akron, by any chance? Ma's cousin married a man from Akron. You might be acquainted. Name of Wilkerson, Harold Wilkerson, in the construction business?"

"I'm from Columbus, actually."

She punches open the door. "That near Akron? Stella!" she calls, not waiting for his answer. "I've got a young man here to help you out."

A brown face smiles at him above a steamy pot. "Columbus!" Stella declares. "You came all the way down from Columbus to work at Three Square Meals?"

Time Out

It doesn't add up.

Henrietta has Val on her mind. How, when he first came in, he'd plunked himself down in a back booth before anyone had time to clear it. What was the burning hurry? He's been with her two days now, and she's still turning him over in her mind.

She didn't press for references, though she knows better, didn't even ask his last name, though he offered it on his own. Hagen—a nice enough name. It's his real one: he dropped his driver's license yesterday and she caught enough of a glimpse to see that it matched. He's awful pale. Jailhouse pale? she wonders. But a fugitive from justice wouldn't be so free-handed with his name. The other thing she learned was that his license was from New York, not Ohio. Could of moved, of course, and not had time to get it fixed.

His age? Hard to guess. Late twenties? Young thirties? Somewheres around there. Small ears. Means stingy—so? So? No great sin in that.

Val Hagen . . . She doesn't even know what the name "Val" is the short of. When Henrietta thinks of him, her first picture is of the back of his head, the high, clean hairline at the nape of his neck, how smooth it is. Unsunned. He's come from the city, she's sure, though maybe not Columbus.

In the city it's no good. Though she's only visited, never lived in a real city, Henrietta knows how it must be. In the city it's hurry up and wait, and nobody cares. People living stacked up, one on top of the other, in buildings that crowd out the sky. You get hurt in the city, people always said. Hurt and hurting back, that's often the way . . .

He's a clean-looking young man, and quiet, this Val, but she's pretty sure he's in trouble. Maybe not with the law, but some kind of trouble, some burden of the heart. She'd picked up something from him right away, something that said: watch your step, don't touch, don't come too near.

Could be dangerous. Unwise to take him in. Henrietta's thoughts whirl round and round, making no headway. Here she is priding herself on her gift of discernment—she'd picked up something from him right away, and gone clear against it. And she wouldn't of taken him in but for the fact that she had nothing to lose. The lonesomeness just rolled up out of her at the sight of him. Even without his driver's license, she could tell he was coming from a long ways off.

Today is one of her green days. Green dress, green eye shadow, green button earrings. Lime Rub cologne from a green bottle. Henrietta's given herself an hour off this morning to see the dentist and it feels like a full holiday. Truth to tell, she's felt a holiday coming on ever since she got off work last night. At her prayers, she caught herself saying, "Lord, I am a swimmer," when what she meant was "sinner."

And even if it takes an hour and a half, Stella can manage. Stella and the new help. Val's quick and able, Henrietta can vouch for that. One of the fastest stackers she's seen and he hasn't chipped anything yet. Hasn't missed an addition, either. Most nearly all the routines he got down the first day, pat. Already, he's smarting off to the customers: "First refills on the house. Anything after—refills, freshen-ups, half-cups, warm-ups, just a few drops—it's all twenty cents." Like he's been waiting on customers for years and years and knows all their little ways.

It's such a nice day, everybody's feeling it. On the corner of Main Street, there's a man with a bullhorn making a buzz: "Would you like to say hello to Stan Larick?" Not particularly. The election for mayor won't be coming up for months, but Larick is a long shot trying to make up for it by hard work. So what can she do? Henrietta sticks out her hand and says, "Good luck to you." And they've got something going, a little stir.

Such a pretty day! There goes May and Tom Stowe. The old May Musick. You can tell it's those two a mile down the road by how they sway together walking. Tom has a permanent swag to his left, May to her right, from leaning in to Tom's good ear.

How they've all changed . . . Time has dazed them, bleached and blurred, burned off the clean lines of difference between one and another. At the thirty-fifth reunion of Sam Houston High, they had to wear name cards, and the girls printed their maiden names on them in big block letters, for they had all grown strange. They'd pinned on old photos, too, from the class yearbook. Without those tags, Sam Plemons said, they might not of been able to recognize a one of them.

And speaking of the devil, isn't that Sam in the blue pickup? She's not real sure, he's gone by so fast. Henrietta wants a cigarette so bad, it comes over her in a whoosh, the sudden hunger for it sucks all the air from her throat. It happens like this every time, catching up with her when she's thinking of days gone by. Even though she quit twelve years ago and hasn't touched a butt since, there'll come a moment like this.

But she's not going back on it. When she quit, she quit for all time.

She couldn't of done it without God's help, of course. For years, she'd been praying over it, putting herself down on the Daughters of the King prayer list, telling her friends to pray for her, too, but not really ready to give it up. It happened finally at Gladys Posey's wedding party. Henrietta had been stuffing herself—they all had. There was a crowd and no place to sit down. They were all hanging around the table with the cakes, and when she tried to pluck a cigarette from the pack she always kept open in her purse—must of been the finger of the Lord!—she couldn't make it budge.

She can remember it clear as the day before yesterday. She dug in again—same thing!—she couldn't get a grip on it. Then she heard a voice coming from a man standing with his back to her. Nobody she knew. He was so big he seemed to blot out half the table. "Woman, you'll never smoke again," he said, and Henrietta knew he was talking to her. Well! She snatched up that pack right then and there, ripped it wide open, lit up and took a pull on it. A long swallow of pure spite, deep and slow.

And thought nothing more of any of it. Rest of the day she was so busy fixing dinner, and then dishes, and then one thing and another, that she didn't sit down once. Didn't touch a cigarette; it never crossed her mind.

Day after, she was clearing a table. It was near quitting time. In one of the ashtrays she found a pack of Lucky Strikes, pretty well mashed, but with one cigarette forgotten in its folds, and she just couldn't stand it. So she sat herself down and reached for that pack with both hands. Then she lit up, leaned back and inhaled for all she was worth, waving the cigarette like a wand high in the air, for the joy of it. Smoked it right down to the last button; she still has a scar from where she scorched her thumb on it.

That was February 16, 1974. On that very same night she dreamed she was smoking a cigarette that must of been a foot and a half long; it was wonderful. And that was her farewell to smoking. She never picked up another cigarette, even when her mouth and nose burned with needles for weeks.

But here it is, next to CROP INSURANCE.

The door to the waiting room is open, the office door closed. She can hear Dr. Purcell rattling things and singing inside there, though she can't pick out the words. Then she latches onto the tune. It's "Saved by the Blood," one of her favorites. Dr. Purcell is a Christian dentist. That's how he lists himself in the yellow pages, and it's so, Henrietta wouldn't have any other kind. He's also a gentleman. When her mouth is full, he never orders her to "spit" like other dentists do; it's always, "Do you want to empty?" instead. A Christian and a gentleman. But, of course, the two always go together.

Henrietta sits down noisily to let Dr. Purcell know she's arrived. The singing stops, starts again, a tune new to her. Helping herself to the magazine on top of the stack –it's called *Virtue*–she fans through the pages. An ad for engagement rings leaps to her eye. DIAMOND BRIGHT FOREVER. Not true: nothing on earth is forever. Everything breaks in time. When Charlie was so sick, the skin rolled off his back. Whole patches of it. She was giving him a back rub with lotion, some ordinary hand lotion, Pond's or Nivea, that she brought with her to the hospital, and was rubbing very gently–when the skin came off in her hands. "It happens," the doctor explained, "it wasn't your doing. When a person's been very sick . . ."

The ad says: SHE IS THE ONLY GIRL IN THE WORLD FOR HIM. The girl is all in white, misty; she's smiling into the glittery leaves around her. They're chilly, damp green, the new green of winter wheat. HE IS THE ONLY BOY . . . Henrietta skips on past. More ads. A white-haired lady with "regularity problems" pressing a finger to her lips. She's trying to hush a parrot perched on her shoulder, who's blatting out something he shouldn't. Henrietta had a parrot once, way back when she first met Charlie. The parrot's name was "Treasure." All Henrietta could get her to say was "Good girl!", yet Charlie taught her to say "Whoopee!" and "I'm Treasure" the very first time they met. He had a gift that way.

More ads. A cake recipe catches her eye. It's called a BETTER-THAN-SEX CAKE. Henrietta has her doubts about that, but when she runs her finger down the list of ingredients—crushed pineapple, custard, banana, coconut, lots of Cool Whip—she has to admit that it does sound real tempting.

But now Dr. Purcell is ready for her, standing in the doorway, flashing his perfect smile, his neat, square teeth pearly white. He carries Henrietta's purse over to a side table, then tips her back in the long chair. Stuffing her mouth with rolls of cotton, he murmurs a little prayer for the filling.

"Easy . . . safe and pleasant" is what Henrietta hears, and the ending—"in Jesus' name." Henrietta says "Ah-men" into the cotton, where it is absorbed entirely. Then Dr. Purcell takes the syringe out from its hiding place and slides the needle from its case. Henrietta closes her eyes and for an instant—the pinprick of an instant—sees the eyes of the young man she hired, pale as ice.

She lays back and rests while Dr. Purcell gives her time to numb.

Then he's back; he puts into her hand a little mirror on a stem and angles it to show the red rising between her molars. "Proud flesh!" Dr. Purcell jabs her gums with his metal pick. "Evil, edematous, and full of blood," he mutters darkly. "Pretty soon we're going to have to cut that back." He takes the mirror away: a relief; it's not been pretty. "Have you been flossing?" he asks.

"Trying," is all she can say. She does try. She knows what he is going to say to that, and, sure enough, he does: "You have to do more than try."

Henrietta feels sinful to have so many fillings when Dr. Purcell, as he never tires of reminding her, has never had a one. Sweets are one of Henrietta's main weaknesses, she's the first to admit it. Put a bar of soap in my hand and tell me it's chocolate and I'd eat it, she thinks. But she's given up cigarettes, she's about given up on sex, what else is a body to do?

Did Henrietta know that Clark Gable had to have a complete set of dentures by the time he was thirty? No, she hadn't known, she wouldn't of guessed. She always learns something new from her visits to Dr. Purcell.

"Sorry to destroy that image," he says.

No, you aren't—not a bit sorry, Henrietta can't help feeling. Anyway, it's been how many years since she last thought of Clark Gable?

The way back seems twice as long as it was coming. That's the novocaine wearing thin, the heat, sticky-bright like honey. Her blouse clings unpleasantly. If it's this hot in early June, no telling what August will be like. She'll have to start up the air conditioner soon, the fans won't be enough. What with the hard winter past, the new refrigerator, and now this, expenses are steadily mounting up.

Back in, it's a sight. Val's scarce. Out running an errand, Stella says. Stella's been hanging out the order window—that's where she was when Henrietta surprised her. Too busy making bug eyes at the customers to notice that the pie safe's open and the sugar dispensers need filling. Here Henrietta had been feeling so upbeat! She stoops to gather a wadded napkin on the floor, thinking how it goes to show what Ma always told her: "Sing before breakfast and you'll cry before noon." Well, and it's true.

In the kitchen, the washer's humming, and the radio beside it, playing to itself. Henrietta checks the refrigerator, the pantry and the clipboard with the order list posted on the pantry door. One of those golden oldies is playing—"Nobody wants to do nothin'. Ever'body waitin' for somefin' "—she's already wise on that! They're running late on the lunch preparations. Butter's hard froze—it should of been standing out softening, ready for slicing into pats. Nobody's started the batter for chicken-fried steak; the mixing bowl she left out to remind Stella is idling on the counter there, empty.

"Waitin' for a prize from the big quiz show—"

Henrietta snaps off the radio. She means to have a word with Stella.

But first to make her rounds.

"How you doing?" . . . "You decided yet?" . . . "Everything all right here?" . . . "Tried our pineapple-strawberry cup?" Henrietta moves from table to table. And what's this? Leroy waiting in one of the booths, beating time with his fingers on the linoleum tabletop. It's squeaky clean, not even a glass or a place setting on it. No saying how long he's been sitting there. "Anybody helping you?" she asks. He shrugs. "You need a menu?"

"I looked, but I forget. Eggs is what I wanted. I guess."

"Over easy?"

"I guess. Not raw, anyhow."

Then she notices Father Gilvary sitting alone at a table for four. He's stooped over his coffee, his white collar undone. Looks like plastic–those things must be cutting. And hot. People usually greet him when he comes in and he greets them back, folks get along pleasantly in Durance, but what all can you say? Hot enough for you? Cool enough for you? How's business? Heavens, how long can you go on trying to be nice when effort is all you feel? But they do go on trying, anyway. And wherever he chooses to sit finally, a polite hush falls on the tables around him, everybody minding their manners for a little while–until they forget he's there. He used to come in with his own bunch and they had themselves a lively time. Now it's mostly by himself. They're all getting on at his church, to hear tell, dying off fairly regular.

Must be hard for them, Henrietta thinks. Durance is a strong church town, but Baptist, Methodist, Holiness, Pentecostal, Church of Christ, Precious Blood–anything but Roman or Campbellite. Too much good sense in these parts; neither one ever did take root in Jayroe County. And, praise the Lord, they never would!

Still . . . you can't help feeling something for the old man in his stiff tight collar, he's human too.

He's picking away at what's left of his cinnamon twist (same thing every morning), his hands unsteady. The way he glances up and reaches for his check says something to Henrietta. Something in the angle of his neck that's too eager and too slow, he's leaning too long after the action passes. Henrietta knows what his worry is: his eyes are failing. It just hits her how it is.

Pastoral Care

"Now about this glory business," Dr. Stas begins, "the rosy light—the halo effect. The halos are glaucoma. Your eyes are filled with fluid. It's like when you've been too long in the swimming pool—I don't know if you've ever had that experience—it's the same haloing when you look at the lights. You follow me?"

Father Gilvary nods.

"The rosy light—that's the cataract. What happens is that the cataracts absorb rays from the short end of the spectrum, the blues, the violets and so on, and you may have become more aware of rays from the red end of the spectrum. Most patients don't notice the change, but working, as you do, under stained glass, you're liable to be more conscious of it."

"A warmer world," Father Gilvary proposes.

"Yes, well, for a little while. The progress of your glaucoma will put an end to that. Your peripheral vision will dim first. When the glaucoma takes over it will look like a visor being pulled down over your eyes. Or like fog closing in."

Dawn, then twilight . . . it takes a moment to register.

"I'm so sorry. If you'd come in earlier maybe, then we might have . . ."

Might . . . maybe . . . if . . . They sit knee to knee in the darkened room. Too close for comfort. Father Gilvary is resting his chin on a frame that cups his entire face. Dr. Stas is beaming a small, intensely bright light into one eye, then the other, when there blazes forth a vision: twice: the stark, necrotic branches of a tree—against a sky on fire. It is as though his eyes have been seared with a branding iron: a winter tree in each.

Darkness follows, like a salve.

Dr. Stas clears his throat.

The darkness is no longer a relief. It is full, not empty; ghosted, not silent. Charged with a clinging moisture, a pressure, the air tells him that Dr. Stas is an inch away and leaning ever closer.

Face breath—is how Father Gilvary explains it to himself, the clouding of presence, a kind of knowing. Even stone breathes, he's learned. If he closes his eyes and listens with his skin, he can almost hear it. It's not really hearing, or touching, or looking, but some mixed sensing, a sixth sense perhaps, formed of these.

Then the doctor tells him to lift his head; the chin support folds away, the face breath evaporates. The doctor himself backs off, still seated on his stool, two blunt feet and four little wheels scuttling across the floor. Lights return, and Dr. Stas says something about facing losses as we all must. "I don't know any other way to go but older, do you?" he says. To which Father Gilvary replies, "Of course—of course not."

Your sufferings are added because they were lacking, the appropriate text comes to mind. *You fill up a measure. You do not pour something that overflows.* But it does overflow, sometimes.

"We are all going blind," says Dr. Stas, "and if we live long enough, we will. Now I'm going to give you some drops to help ease the pressure. There may be some side effects—stinging, reddening, pupil dilation—the nurse will tell you exactly what to expect. Call me—at any time—if you have any questions. I expect you are making plans."

Plans?

He will take the days one by one and see his obligations through ordinary time at least. Surely he can manage to hold on for a few more months.

Too bright. Father Gilvary leaves the dim cave coolness of the doctor's office and steps out into the dazzle of day. Already, the heat is palpable, his collar chafing. One step, then another. He places his feet with care, the sun, spoked like a monstrance, brassy before his eyes. He shifts his case to his left hand.

Coming near. If he half-closes his eyes and practices,

he can feel the obstruction of the free passage of air, the clogged warmth of cement, along his right side, the wall, the west wall of the hospital. He takes the wide steps, four —remember to remember that—then the double doors, outer and inner. The corridor is easy, one straight shot—he knows his way with eyes shut.

In room 28, one of the beds is empty. There's a newcomer occupying the other bed. Father Gilvary hesitates in the doorway.

"It isn't what you think, Father," the man explains. "Mike was transferred out of Intensive a couple of days ago. Should be home by now."

"Ah."

"That's good news, isn't it?"

"Yes, of course," Father Gilvary affirms, then mumbles something about being on his way.

"Got a minute?"

"Sure."

"You can talk to me, Father." When the man attempts to sit up, Father Gilvary sees that he is tethered to a machine. "Or do you have to be Catholic to talk to you?"

"Of course not." Father Gilvary steps well inside. "Be happy to." There is no chair, so he stands, rather stiffly, case in hand, a short distance from the bed. "My name's Gilvary—Tom Gilvary."

"Mine's Jake."

"As in Jacob?"

Jake nods, and Father Gilvary wonders how to go on from here. He stands at attention, a regimental straightness. Stares at the Venetian blind: too bright, then at its reflection on the floor, where light and shadow are laid in stripes, like a fence thrown down. In the quiet, he hears the tumbling of his own heart, he's tumbling, the ground yielding, and he needs to reach out, to clasp– To grasp hold. Yet he knows the floor is firm, his bearing upright, rigid, unbending. His enforced stillness is as great an effort as uphill running, his breath as short. For, in truth, he longs to bend, to lean, to turn to Jake, this perfect stranger, and cry out: "Help me–I'm going blind." A yearning so fierce that Father Gilvary can feel it actually pulsing in his throat, a small, baffled chiming, not yet sound.

He coughs harshly, twice.

The moment passes. To his relief and sorrow, Father Gilvary realizes that nothing, after all, has happened. He has given nothing away.

"My prognosis," Jake begins, "it isn't good."

Father Gilvary sighs: they are on familiar ground. "And your family?" he asks.

"Separated. Years ago."

Father Gilvary waits for more detail. It is not forthcoming. "You could call them, even so," he suggests. "Even after years of not talking, you'd be surprised how the old connections hold. I've seen it happen. Sometimes it takes that long–years–a decade, even–for the old resentments to let go."

Jake leans back heavily, lets his eyes close. "You've got visits to make, Father, and I'm beat. I don't know what I was thinking of."

"I'll come by again," says Father Gilvary.

His next stop is a little ways up the hall, near the nursing station. No one to ask, so he peers into the shadows of room 22. All still . . . an even, purling sound. Good: John seems to be sleeping. He's breathing unassisted, first time in a long time.

The stop coming up now is the one he dreads. He knows what to say, and has tried, but cannot go on with the prescribed phrases. As a young priest, he'd have done better. He's seen too much since. When Pete put it to him last time: "Why me, Father?", he'd been forced to admit: "I don't know. I wish I knew."

And today–soon as he knocks–Pete turns to him, his face flushed. "I don't want any of that holy holy!"

"I'll just sit with you a bit, if I may."

Welcome or not, Father Gilvary proceeds to visit, perching, though not settling, on the one available chair, balancing his case on his knees. The television is going full blast, high up, on the wall facing the bed. Something about total commitment to yogurt. Pete has turned over on his side, one arm thrown over his face, exposing the blackness of his armpit, a sudsing mass of hair.

How young he is, how abundantly, indecently, young–

The room is full of cards, candy and flowers. Cruel, Father Gilvary thinks, the sweets he can't eat, the flowers heartlessly bright, the get well cards cheery with lies. And the things people say to the dying! "Tomorrow," or "See you soon," or "I can't wait." Or "I nearly died." They talk fast, their voices jostle and push. The world is cruel, yes, he knows. Or simply careless.

"Save your prayers, Father. I'm not taking Communion."

"It would ease you," Father Gilvary says, tapping

the case with his fingertips. "It would, you know. I've seen it happen, time and time again."

"Not with me," says Pete.

Probably true, Father Gilvary thinks to himself, if he's determined that it won't. Just then, strangely, there's a call for him over the loudspeaker. From Admissions—would he come down?

"In a few minutes," he answers.

"You might as well go now," Pete puts in.

"If that's the way you're feeling–"

"And don't tell me you're going to pray for me."

"Pray for me, Pete," the words are wrung from him.

"Now, Granma–" In Admissions, there's a struggle going on.

"You'll tire yourself out," one of the nurses says soothingly. "Do I look like somebody you know?"

No answer but the sound of chapped lips kissing air.

It's an old woman they picked up in the bus terminal. They've tied her to a wheelchair with twisted strips of sheet, but she keeps arching her back, trying to break free. Her bare feet are swollen and cracked, her face deeply seamed. Her hair is dyed a shocking blood red; it is white at the roots.

"Sena, can you tell us where you're from?"

She can't, or she won't. She's in a hospital gown; she's been processed: stripped, washed, her body features noted, her skin felt. Her teeth have been counted: the nurse tells him that she has nine. Her scalp has been examined and treated with benzo-benzo-eight. For lice.

Her name, Sena Petersen, is printed on adhesive taped to her wrist.

Father Gilvary asks Sena if she wants to talk to him, perhaps in private, but she doesn't answer, only stares at him, her eyes wide with shock.

"Know what day it is, Sena?" the nurse asks. She has plaited the patient's hair in a single braid and is tying it up in a ribbon of gauze.

"Can you remember what day this is?" the nurse persists.

She cannot.

"Why don't you talk to Father here?"

"He's not my father!"

Father Gilvary tries to explain, but Sena turns her face away from him and starts to weep hoarsely. "What did I ever do to any of you?" she accuses. "This is some beauty treatment!"

"You have my number?" Father Gilvary asks the senior nurse. He is eager to be off. He's fairly sure that Sena is Lutheran—Petersen is a Scandinavian name—and that she will remember this when she begins to remember again.

The small tan brick of Saint Jude's has been Father Gilvary's home for sixteen years now. It's a contemporary church, flat-roofed for economy's sake. The spire is short, ladderlike, hung with four bells in descending order of size. The bells are rarely used. There's a tape he plays whenever chimes are requested—it's easier.

Father Gilvary longs for the lofty spires and high

vaultings of the churches in his youth; he misses that sense of stretching, of reaching. Churches nowadays look more like gyms or social halls, which they mostly are.

Still . . . Saint Jude's has been home to Father Gilvary for a long time now. It had been his wish to grow old, to die in harness, here. Even with his full sight, he'd no longer have the energy for starting up again in a new parish. Now he'll have his wish–but differently. He'll remain at Saint Jude's for as long as he can hold out.

Opening the church doors, all the pent odors wash over him–old beeswax, stale incense, lilies overripe, long since blackened into soil. Vanished, not perished. His eyes move–from baptistry to altar, to the place where he is now standing, where he meets the entering coffin–the completed circle of a life. He does not see, so much as feel, his way down the center aisle, the worn, beloved path, the Blessed Mother on the gospel side, Saint Joseph on the epistle side, the faithful sanctuary lamp glowing like an ember. Passing the tabernacle nestled in shadow, he dips down slowly on one knee.

Through the sacristy to the kitchen. What for lunch? Rattling around in the pantry, he always has the same thought: ought to hold a fire sale, all these pots and pans. This rectory belonged to the old church; there've been no renovations here, no changes, only decades of accumulation. That yellow can of beef stew might be twenty years old; it was here when Father Gilvary moved in. Those gray and brittle bay leaves in their bottle. The spices, row upon row of canisters and small flasks, like the rectory chairs in their dustiness and needless duplication, speak to him of a procession of tenants before his time. Speak to him of transience.

Tuna! That's what he wants. Father Gilvary sketches a benediction over the unopened can. He is famished.

He pores over the parish accounts while he eats, using a magnifying glass to check the figures. The sausage dinner they held in May netted nearly two thousand dollars. That will barely cover utilities. The Waring property should bring in something, but it's too early to even guess how much. The will has yet to be probated.

CCD dues—not worth recording. There have been no confirmations for the past two years. None. The only baptism has been Rosie Macfee's grandson. That was last summer. Her daughter came into town to show off the new baby, and Rosie roped him into doing it.

Clearly, Saint Jude's has no purchase on the future. Father Gilvary has seen it coming for a long time. His people are, none of them, getting any younger. It's the same pattern in most small towns. Look at Wayside. The young people—who can blame them?—clear out as soon as they're able. Saint Jude's will go the way of small churches with aging parishioners: almost certainly it will be downgraded to mission status. The priest in Letsem City will stop by once every week or so.

Two o'clock. Father Gilvary picks up his mail, doubles back to the kitchen to retrieve his magnifying glass, and settles in at his desk. Oh, dear—here's one he suspects he knows the text of by heart . . . Restore the Tridentine Mass, do not allow the Body of Christ to be taken in the hand, only on the tongue, bring back the beautiful long habits and respect for Vocations. There's more. The pages are turning, the Revelations unfolding as foretold–the Tribulation, the winnowing of the earth is at hand– Now who–? No one is in the parish, thank goodness. Billings, Ontario–must be a chain letter. Shrine of Mary Sustainer of Mothers. Fit right in in Durance, though. Oh, mercy. It's coming. First a global war, then comets. Finish it off. In case the first wasn't enough. Before war breaks out, the entire world will see a sign of warning in the sky, as was foretold in the apparitions of– what?–starts with a "C," no, "G," can't make it out, someplace, Spain in 1965.

Brother!

What else? A religious supply catalog featuring "shepherd shirts for summer," the latest issue of *Our Sunday Visitor,* and–oh! On the envelope, he spots the small pineapple-shaped chancery seal–ORA PRO NOBIS–disarmingly modest, surely the most modest in the nation. He lifts the letter close to the lamp. The light, simple lamplight, seems astonishingly brilliant.

The letter turns out to be a reminder of something he has not forgotten. Clergy Day, the annual gathering of priests at Lake Watooska, is coming up at the end of June; this is his second notice. Fraternally yours in Christ–

Father Gilvary tells himself for a second time that he'll think about it later, knowing full well that he won't. Simply hasn't the heart for it any longer. He knows what he will find: the ranks of familiar faces thinning, Jim Titus, the young vicar general, a company man, holding forth, and smiling, smiling. He is all too familiar with Jim's agenda: Diocesan Development Fund, new buildings, the latest wheelings and dealings in real estate, the list of approved altar wines . . . Father Gilvary is tired of always being the one to break in with objections. "But what about prayer? Why do we never talk about prayer?" Young Jim is considered a model priest–his twenty-some-inch waist a real boost to vocations in the chancery view. And an utter fool in the eyes of Father Gilvary.

Nevertheless, Father Gilvary draws his calendar to him and makes careful note of the date. Then turns the pages back to today, checking what's left on his schedule. Not a whole lot. A middle-aged couple due in for marriage counseling. That's down for two-thirty. Parish council at seven. The matter under discussion, the burning issue, is finances. Bingo has been the only steady solution. The irony is that so many Baptists, forbidden to gamble by their own churches, are the ones who turn out for it. Baptists are keeping the Catholics in business.

Already, at quarter of seven, Sue Penders is at the door. "To help you set up the coffee," she says. Meaning: she'll take care of it. "Let me see what the milk situation is." An excuse to be poking around in the refrigerator.

"How old is this, do you suppose?"–she's pointing to a round of cheese he could swear he's never laid eyes on before; it's furred with a green mold. And now she's inspecting a plate stacked with dark chunks of something; she takes and pinches one: "And what might these have been? They're turning to wood!" Father Gilvary cannot recall–might have been brownies? fudge? Mary or Martha, some doting parishioner– Sue Penders, herself?–must have dropped by with it. Couldn't be Sue's–she'd recognize the plate. How long has it been sitting around? He has no idea. "And this!" She stoops to retrieve a bowl from way back of the middle shelf. Together, they peer over a graying jellied mass in a deep dish. "The cover must have fallen off," he explains. "Why it looks that way." Whatever it was . . . Congealed broth would be his best guess. Mushrooms, and barley, and–? Okra? He hates to throw food out. "You have to remember," he smiles lamely, "I'm a professional bachelor." He has said this before in similar circumstances. Many a time. Sue isn't buying it. "Really, Father! I know you have a lot on your mind, but when was the last time you defrosted? When did you last even look inside?"

By the time parish council comes around, Father Gilvary is bent with weariness. Fortunately, nothing much is required of him beyond the opening and closing prayers – "May our coming together begin with You, move with You, and through You be happily ended"–his all-purpose invocation for ordinary occasions. He is expected to put in a word now and then, and he does, but the meeting could continue nearly as well without him. There's something he's been meaning to say, but he's forgotten; he'll have to wait for it to come back to him.

"If we ran Bingo six nights a week we could raise four hundred dollars a night," Dick Stevens insists. "All we need is forty thousand to build a hall. I've asked around and those are the going bids."

Forty thousand! Unreal! They are dreaming, of course. Father Gilvary sighs and holds his peace. When they cease to dream they will cease to be.

Betty Fisher asks if you have to have a certain number of rest rooms to accommodate a certain number of people, and Dick says that they are not yet at the point where they have to worry about details like that. If they tie into the parish hall, people can use the rest rooms there. Of course they would have to add on eventually, but they are not yet at the point where they need to begin combing through the municipal code.

They aren't anywhere remotely near that point. Around the long table where they sit, the air is thick, and darkening. Sue is tracing the grain of the wood, doodling loops within loops with her forefinger. Reading by finger-light . . . Father Gilvary feels himself drifting off, his lips moving. He bites his underlip: *watch it.* Soon be dreaming out loud. If he doesn't watch it. *Fingerlight* . . . what does it mean? Why does the word fill him with such misgiving? It was something the nurse said to him this morning after the eye exam, something about learning braille, brought it to mind. A course being given this summer, in Letsem City. He said he'd think about it, meaning he wouldn't. Not yet. Can't focus, can't take it in.

It's hard to keep his eyes propped open. If only he could concentrate! Is this what it will be like in the days to come? Dozing through the time remaining, drowsing in daylight, always drifting or fighting the drift, the steady, resistless slide into oblivion? Waking–sleeping–will they be different? How different? The voices of the parish council drone on, the long blades of the ceiling fan cast revolving shadows on the table beneath. Round and round to no effect. It is as though a veil has fallen, the very air a drapery. Muffled in its folds are seven familiar faces, in-substantial now as clouds.

Dick says a breezeway will have to be built under the power lines to connect the new Bingo hall with the old parish hall. Which brings Sam Mattney back to the point he made earlier: "Better to lease a building, rather than tie up forty thousand dollars to build one. There are plenty of vacant buildings in town." Dick says he'll look into that; it's not out of the question. Tom Gerrish suggests that Dick call Earl Alred's son, who would know about empty buildings. Father Gilvary agrees that it can't hurt for Tom to ask. Dick announces that he'll take care of it himself, and Tom falls into a miffed silence. There are moments in life, Father Gilvary reflects, when you experience the full burden of your choices. This is one of them.

Small business, then the closing benediction. Father Gilvary remembers what it was he wanted to say at the beginning of the meeting. It was about Father John Kenny, the pastor he succeeded here at Saint Jude's, now at death's door. "He's at his sister's house in Lawton if any of you want to write to him. But there may not be time for that. Please pray, all of you, that God may grant him a peaceful passage to the eternal kingdom."

A flurry of hands as they sign off in the name of the Father, the Son, and the Holy Spirit, then Sue Penders turns to him and says, "You're not looking yourself, Father."

"It's the heat. What I need is a good night's sleep," he assures her, seeing them all to the door. He checks that the lights are out, then stumbles back through the rectory in darkness.

A good night's sleep . . . How did it go? *A restful night and a perfect death* was what they used to pray for at

Compline, at day's end. He fills the cup on his bedside table, checks his alarm, then picks up his breviary. Although he can no longer read it with ease, the familiar heft of it comforts his hands. With care, he moves the markers one day forward—in case he dies tonight and is discovered in the morning. He makes a quick act of contrition.

Darkness enters him. There is no quiet in it. He hears voices—Dick, Tom, Sue, Betty, then Dr. Stas saying, "Goodnight, Father," then Pete and Jake, even Sena, joining in. *Father* . . . the word light as two falls of a feather. Father? Of what?

Payday

On the days he gets up early enough, Val likes to walk to work. Walking clears his head, and mornings are the best time for it. Durance Boulevard, the old East-West Highway, is the red light district, and all but deserted in daylight. Life here only begins to pick up after five when the Happy Hour begins.

When Val's late, like today, he rides the bus. It's a quick five, ten-minute run, depending on the driver. Sometimes he spends more time waiting for the bus to arrive than actually riding.

KATE'S FEED AND SPIRITS . . . he watches the sights go by. They pass TOOT n' TOTUM. Open all hours and they sell just about everything—milk, beer, screwdrivers, chewing tobacco, detergent, *Playboy, Penthouse,* you name it. Frozen burritos, even, to be zapped to life in the microwave. They pass rows of ghost motels, some renting by the hour, some by the month, some—leaning, but still standing —are past renting on any basis, blasted by wind, bleached down to their gray wood bones. Ought to pull them down, what's left of them. One quick blaze would redeem the lot. The land has to be worth something . . .

They pass the arcaded SILVER SADDLE LOUNGE. A real rip-off, as Val can testify. He went in for a drink after a long day at the meat packers and watched a naked woman ride a kid's tricycle round and round the horseshoe-shaped bar. The tricycle was painted silver and the men watching kicked at the wheels to slow the woman down. Freckled blonde with hard eyes, she looked like a girl Val knew once. Some Janette or Suzanne, fancy name like that. But they all look the same, don't they? Val stared at her splayed, blubbery bubs—and scrammed. Left half a pitcher of fresh draw, untouched.

There are four other passengers riding the bus and they all seem to know each other, well enough to pass the time of day, anyhow. One of them's sloshed. He's greased up quite a bit, you can smell it.

"You look a little sick today," one of the sobers says to the drunk, "eyes kind of bloodshot."

"I was born that way. Scared my ma half to death."

"What did you say your job was?"

"Drinking. It's a big job." He wants to be let off at the Big Dipper. "There she is!" he slaps the window, staggers to his feet. "That's a church," the driver corrects

Payday

him. "Cantcha read? Seven Lampstands Pentecostal, and it's closed."

"I'll open her up!" says the drunk, lurching to the exit.

Val still reads the want ads, it helps kill time. There's more want than work in Durance, he's learned.

WANTS KITTEN/ WANTS PUPPY/ PUPPY LOST/ WANTS CHAIR/ WANTS HOUSE/ WANTS TRAILER/ NEEDS NURSE/ WANTS BALER/ WRONG COAT/ JACKET, WATCH LOST/ SHOES LOST/ BILLFOLD LOST/ EARRING LOST/ DOES IRONING/ DOES HAULING/ WEED WIPER/ KEEPS CHILDREN/ WANTS RANCH WORK/ CRUSTBUSTER (FOLDUP DRILL)/ COMBINE SALVAGE SALE/ BALER/ BALER/ WIRE BALER/ TRACTOR PARTS/ WILL RAISE CANARY/ WANTS CHILD/ ROOM TO SHARE/ SEEKS CHUM/ WOULD CORRESPOND/ LOVELY LADY/ LONELY WIDOW/ HEARTBROKEN/ SMALL TREES . . .

He's nearly fifteen minutes late and it's one of those days, right from the start. Some hayseed he's never laid eyes on before blows in and asks for a pig-hip sandwich. Val says he's never heard of any such thing, and surely not for breakfast.

"You should of. It's made with fresh pork and a secret sauce. And it's delicious any old time of day."

"We sure don't have it," says Val.

"How about raisin pie?"

It's too early for putting out pie, though they've got some slices left over from yesterday in the fridge. But no raisin. Val offers what they have: custard cream and cherry.

"Just have this yen for raisin pie. I haven't aten any for so long. Guess I'll just have to go out and find myself some," and he walks out.

"That doesn't look like a satisfied customer to me," Henrietta remarks.

"Well," says Val, "he isn't." That's all he's going to explain. He doesn't owe her anything.

A rushed morning. It's after ten before Val gets to sit down to his own breakfast. He takes a booth he hasn't yet found time to clear, littered with leftover grits, and morsels of biscuit and cream gravy—this morning's breakfast special. The ashtray is warted with wads of chewing gum.

They must have come in from across the street because they've left behind one of those pale blue IN MEMORIAM leaflets. Val's chucked out quite a number of them. This one's in memory of Don Parker, BORN: JULY 2, 1915 IN ARCADE, OKLAHOMA, ENTERED INTO REST: and the date is today—which reminds Val that today is payday. Henrietta promised him time off to get to the bank before three.

It took a couple of days before Val learned that Three Square Meals was better known as "Henrietta's Cemetery Restaurant," and that half of their customers stopped in on their way back from burying somebody. Val doesn't know why he failed to realize this from the start; he'd seen, but not registered, the hearse pulled up in front the very first time he stepped through the door. It only made sense to him after the fact.

They do a lot of talk about burying at the restaurant —why a dirt farmer should or shouldn't want to lie in marble, whether a married couple should lie side by side, or stacked. Side by side is the preferred way.

Around two, the boy they call "Cleat" comes in for a Coke. He's the one with the handouts and the eyeglasses. Born loser, if ever there was one. He walks like a stork, like some geeky bird. Sets this little stack of papers on the counter and, when Val comes by to take his order, hands him one. It's INVITE HIM INTO YOUR HEART, same as before. Post office box number, the same.

"I saw this before," says Val, sliding it back to him.

Cleat shrugs, doesn't insist. "God told me to do it," he whispers.

"That it? Just the Coke?" Val asks.

"For me–I could hear it," Cleat says. " 'Write this, and give it out wherever you go,'–that's what I heard. If you'd of been standing beside me, you wouldn't of heard it."

"You can bet on that," says Val.

Val has three quarters of an hour to cash his check. It's hot, and the dust is blowing. His eyelids are raw, he's breathing in sand; even his earholes are gritted with it.

Inside, the bank is cool. The air must be filtered, so smooth and silken. Val readies three scraps of paper in his hand. His paycheck, driver's license for name identification, the address of the place where he is now living and of his present place of employment–with these he is armed against the voice that says, *Your memory was better then, wasn't it?* And his own answer: *I don't remember.*

The voices move through the air, but only Val hears them. When the teller stared at him that was only because his lips must have been moving.

Everything's in order, but she keeps glancing up at his face and, once, to the teller alongside, as if double-checking. Val tries not to stare back, yet not to avoid her eyes. He reads the handwritten sign she's tacked up on the wall of her booth:

LUCY BAIR

    LOST CHECK #375

LEW OWENS

DON'T CASH ANYTHING

There's a photo under the warnings. Kind they do for engagement notices in the Sunday papers: a man and a woman (looks like this one), standing ear to ear, his shoulder jumbled into hers, their hair mixed together. Matching tilts to their heads, like question and answer. And the same tuck to their smiles—identical—like they're biting down on the same thing. Tasty, so far.

But now she (the woman, here, live, in front of him) is dishing out a stack of twenties, the ice on her ring flashing. He's clear—in one way, he's clear.

Better keep his name off his door and letterbox, though. As Val folds the bills in halves and stashes them in his wallet, he reflects that he'll soon be paying bills again. The world has a tag on him—a hook.

9

Are You Ready?

In her mind's eye, Henrietta sees the saints of God floating up like paper kites to meet the Lord in the air. They are taking off with her dresses–the reds, the pinks, the yellows, the aqua blue–as she rattles the hangers, hunting for her Wednesday drab go-to-prayer-meeting outfit. Someday, maybe soon, before the trump sounds, she'll let all her glad rags go.

But here it is: navy blue, speckled with tiny salt spots, one hanger was latched onto another. Been here all along.

Henrietta's really not much in the mood for prayer meeting tonight. Maybe it will perk her up, though. She's been feeling a perilous lack of conviction these past few days. It's like Brother Shad says: whichever which way you point, your thumb points the other way.

Still grilling. Henrietta notices two dogs at the corner. One heaped on the other. She doesn't want to look and tries to turn her head away, but her eyes are tugged back to them. Why, she can't say. They're mutts, ordinary. The bitch is yellow, the buck spotted white and black. The buck has mounted and the bitch is gazing off at what passes in the street. One eye's squinched shut; the other's fixed smack dab on her. On Henrietta!

The buck reaches, like all he wants in the world is to make a tent, a skin, over her body. The bitch stands and stares out with one dull eye, letting him fasten, cling, do what he will. Old bitch with low drooping dugs. She seems to be winking at Henrietta, some secret they share.

Truth is, Henrietta's losing the hunger, that special hunger. Funny . . . if it left her, then came again at the end. With Charlie it was food hunger, gorging himself like he wanted to take the whole world into him, to taste everything he'd missed out on before. A taste was all he managed to put by. Whittled down to the point-end of nothing, he was; nothing stuck to him then.

Those were the mean, lean days for both of them.

When Charlie died, his friends came over two by two to pay their respects. In twos! One looking out for the other, their wives not trusting her. She wouldn't forget that easy or soon. Or ever.

She'd been a sod widow for over a year. Lonesome, but bearing up, asking the Lord to give her the strength. So lonesome she got all these crazy ideas sometimes. She

thought of becoming a pen pal to somebody in prison, somebody in Huntsville maybe, on Death Row.

Thinking over and over: *Charlie, how could you?*

Then reminding herself, *I shall go to him, but he will not return to me.* Squeezing along, as best as possible, but near desperate. Asking the Lord to bring somebody into her life if that was what He judged right for her, but not really asking, not waiting for his judgment.

Then she knew she had to get out. Any way out– crawling on her knees, highway, byway, any old side way –how did that song go? So she went to bars, to honky tonks. Took men home, too, and lost her heart to a couple of them. Lost out.

Tumbling down the old road to ruin, when she threw herself on the mercy of the Lord once again. Accepted his lordship over her life.

And He lifted her, He lifted her.

Charlie had a little land, quarter of a section, that never had been worth much for cultivation; she leased it to some independent oilmen, and suddenly the royalties began to roll in. Only lasted a couple of months, but that was enough for Henrietta to risk a bid on a restaurant. Best thing she ever did in her whole entire life, she appreciates that now. It's a place to go and say hello to people, if nothing else. Chance to hear a voice, somebody asking: "How you been keeping?" Anything: "My, what a pretty day!" . . . "What do you know?" . . . "Not a whole bunch." It really doesn't matter what. "Thanks for asking." . . . "So long. Be seeing you." . . . "Have a good one." Left to herself, she might of lost her voice, lost the knack of it.

It's nice to step out in the light of early evening, even if it is still hot. And will you look at that sweep of sky! Far as the eye can stretch. Call that what– "majestic?" Sometimes, after gazing up into that wide unwinking sky, that great blue yonder, Henrietta sees Durance as a tiny, dark, ragged patch torn out of the ever-living prairie, sees the whole town–the restaurant, and herself with it, all her disappointments and sorrows–bleaching out into clear air. And if anybody'd ask her how she feels at those moments, she'd have to say about herself what she'd say about the weather: all calm and fair. That doesn't happen often, but it does happen.

Almost there. The white spike, new-painted, of Rooftree Pentecostal Church can be seen from blocks away. The church is sandstone, perched on a little rise of ground, the closest thing they have to a hill in Durance. With open fields on three sides, it truly stands as "a tent in the wilderness," like Brother Shad says it is.

There are many greetings as Henrietta steps inside. She is "Sister Henny" at Rooftree.

Sister Marcy is standing in the foyer right where you come in, showing off a bundle in a pink blanket. Henrietta steps over to have a peek. "All I can see is hair," she says. There's a thatch of it, coal black.

"Got lots of hair," Marcy agrees. "I must of had heartburn the day the Lord dreamed her up."

"How you feeling?" Henrietta asks.

"All right–now. I don't want to do this again for a while, though."

Brother Wes–Wesley Oakes–is checking the pew racks for hymnals, busy fussing all over the place, and doesn't see Henrietta as she slips by. He once sent Henrietta a love letter with his blood pressure on it: 140/80. Just that. Didn't even sign an initial, but she knew who it was from. Must be seventy-five if he's a day; unbent yet, but not so peppy now. Seems to drag a little to the one side when he walks.

Sister Willodene, setting down in front next to Sister Cloteal, looks big-bellied, wasted. That's the cancer eating at her. It's not sickness, they try not to call it sickness at Rooftree; they call it "hard testing" or "a trying of her faith."

Henrietta settles into a center pew. Hot! Air's muzzy with it. She bends down and loosens the back straps of her shoes and tries to stretch her toes. Ooh, that feels soo— Her eye roams over the pulpit and the blackboard on the easel with its drawing of the budget pie. No matter how hard times may be, the biggest slice at Rooftree always goes for missions.

Heat's really something fierce here and the overhead fans aren't much of a help. There are paper fans in the pew racks, though, advertising FATHER & SON; Henrietta helps herself to one. She stares at the painting over the baptistry, a waterfall between trees, hoping it will bring cool thoughts. There might be a face cut in the rock, under the spill, or there might not—she can never decide. You can't tell, that face might even be smiling. The water falls in braids, in thick white folds like velvet, smothering the rocks beneath. Really, it's not at all cooling.

But now Brother Shad is mounting the platform, two steps at a time, and the choir is shuffling in. There's a ripple in the hall, it's electric, everybody tensing up.

Brother Shad is so good you'd think Jesus Christ himself was standing up there with him, leaning over his shoulder, holding a little mike. Suddenly, with no rhyme of reason, Henrietta thinks of Cleat, remembers him a few years back, standing on the post office steps, singing to himself. Rolling his hips like Elvis and strumming an air guitar. He'd spurted up overnight, seemed like, already a man's height; but no substance to him. Legs like one of those tall birds–just stalks. She couldn't help staring at the sight, and he seemed to be staring back, though you never could be sure what his eyes were up to behind those plates of his. He wore his eyeglasses mashed to his face, the earpieces hitched on by an elastic stretched round the back of his head. He never did have any nose to speak of. She recalls a holster on his belt, too. The kind most boys wear for knives, but all Cleat carried was a pen and pencil in his. Always keeping things attached, trying to fasten them to himself, like he was afraid they might float off.

He'd probably been staring straight through her, away off down the street, waiting for someone or something important to come into view. Seems like he was always waiting, even then.

He's been hanging around the restaurant a lot lately. It's on account of the new help, no question about that. Whenever Henrietta spies him out, he's trailing Val with his eyes. And Val's always short with him. People here learned long ago to let the boy be, just as he was, as the good Lord made him. Val is too new to know that.

But here they all are: the platform is full. Brother Hays is ready for lift-off, standing on tiptoes, arms raised to heaven, index fingers pointed straight up. "He touched me, He touched me," he begins, elbows beating the air like wings, his socks a summery blue, he's lifted–he's airborne– And now, with head sidewise, arms out, he's coasting, gliding, flying high– "with the Holy Ghost!"

"We're gonna pray some folks through to the Holy Ghost tonight!" Brother Shad hollers. Tonight's testifying night; he'll be coming round with the mike in a little minute. "The solution to all our problems is on our knees," he reminds them. "If there'd been ten righteous men in Sodom and Gomorrah, God would have changed the course of world history. Elijah wasn't just blowing smoke when he prayed fire down from heaven to consume his enemies. You wouldn't want him to pray that way in the Panhandle. We're dry enough most nearly all the time."

Then Sister Sally stands up in the cutest little flowerty dress and testifies from her own life. "So many wonderful things," she says, "you pray over them, you lift them up in prayer, and you wait. When it comes, you set in wonderment.

"My biggest wonderment was when my daughter was born. I was the head of my household, you know, my husband was taken . . ." Her voice is all crumbly. "I was always the strongest one . . . and I hated being the strongest one, but I couldn't give it up. I had all this stress, these financial problems. And then the Lord sent a magnificent man to help me. And now I–I'd like to thank the Lord–"

She can't go on.

So Brother Shad steps in. "Praise the Lord for that

magnificent man! Let's give God a big hand," and that sets everybody clapping.

"That's the way, the Lord wants you to get all excited. Any more testimonies?" Brother Shad holds out the mike. "Any more prayer requests? Any more names to be lifted up to God?"

But, no, it's only Sister Sally–a thin harvest tonight. Brother Shad nods to the choir, and Brother Hays takes over, calling out: "One of these days, He's gonna split the clouds. He's gonna take his church. I can't hardly wait–I'm so homesick for Him now." And then the choir just busts out with "I want to be ready." And everybody else chimes in:

"Oh, I

want to be ready–"

And Brother Shad reminds them: "The Lord loves you tonight. Don't you want to be ready?" and Brother Hays and the choir and everybody answers: "I want to be ready!" It's a shouting-singing match, hot and getting hotter, Brother Shad leading with "The Lord loves you tonight. The Lord wants to forgive you of your sins tonight. Tonight He's a God of love, tonight He's a God of mercy–tomorrow He may be a God of wrath. He may be a God of judgment tomorrow."

And they cry out in one voice: "I want to be ready!"

"You better come while you can come to a God of mercy."

"I want to be ready."

"You better come while you can come to a God of love."

"I want to be ready."

"Will you come? Will you come tonight?"

"I want to be ready!"

"Oh, I know, I know in the Holy Ghost that the Lord is dealing with some of you very strongly tonight. I know the Lord is knocking at your hearts. Will you let Him in? You see, I could tell you tonight all you have to do is just accept Jesus Christ as your personal savior and you'd be saved, but I'd be lying to you. That's right. I'm sorry, but I'm not going to lie to you. Now if you want to go back and listen to that mealy-mouthed hireling that stands in the pulpit and tells people that they can go to heaven for two cents, you can do it. But I'm telling you for once you're gonna hear it like it is. You've gotta be baptized in Jesus' name for the remission of sins. Buried in the likeness of his death, risen in the image of his resurrection–that's Romans, chapter six. Not only that: you're got to receive the baptism of fire, the Holy Ghost with evidence of speaking in tongues, or you'll still be here when doomsday comes. You'll still be here! You say, 'Well, that's not the way I believe it.' Well, you better stop believing it your way and start believing it the Bible way! Look up Acts, chapter two, verse thirty-eight. Most of the preachers in the denominal world out there don't even have the Holy Ghost. They're not even qualified to stand behind the pulpit without the Holy Ghost! But that's what we have. We've got a world full of religion–but only just a tiny little bit of salvation out there. I'm not going to mention names and churches–you know who all I'm talking about. Oh, God, the Spirit is moving in this place tonight. Glory to your name, Lord! Glory to your name. Glory to your name, Lord!"

"Glo-ry!"

"Oh, my my my my! Any church that is build upon anything but the solid foundation of the word of God is going to go smash. We're living in a world where people have built their houses, their lives, upon sand—and it's all going smash around them—"

"Lord have mercy!"

"It's all going smash. But let me assure you, before the foundation of the world, the Lord had a plan. Rooftree Pentecostal Church was in that plan. God is the architect here. We're built on a blueprint: we call it the word of God. Look around! There isn't a millionaire among us. Not one of us holds high public office. But Jesus Christ is our city of refuge, our strong tower! The Holy Ghost is head of this church. This is the church of the living God. We're not the most intelligent, the most beautiful or talented. But the Lord has chosen our people, and the Lord has laid his hand upon this church, and the Lord has anointed us. And all the world will be standing on tiptoe to see us when the Lord comes! We are part of the grandest plan, the greatest dream—"

"Praise Him!"

"I'm just an ol' country boy, but look at where He's brought me from, look at where I am!"

"Oh, Graciousness!"

"Turn your eyes on Jesus. Will you? Can you with your anointed imagination see?"

"Jesus! Jesus! Holy Jesus!"

"Would you come? Do you want to be ready when Jesus comes?"

"Oh yes!"

"Do you want to be ready to go out of here?"

"Praise Him!"

"With the saints of God?"

"Yes, yes!"

"If you do, come on down. Kneel at this altar to-night. Saints of God, you feel free to come now."

Their hands are lifted, but nobody's stirring yet. Henrietta would if she could and she calls out "Sweet Jesus!", the words pop softly, unbidden, from her lips. Then she says carefully, "I want to be ready," and knows she isn't ready. Not just yet. Got a dozen things to do. And —it's too interesting now. Could be the devil prompting her, nailing her feet to the ground. Her feet wouldn't budge if she tried.

"You feel free to come, everybody, right now. Let's make this whole church building an altar. Gather round the front, come on. Come on. Oh, Lord, we have need of a real stemwinder tonight! A miracle tonight!"

Only a few are going down—Otis and Ora Burch, Wes Oakes. Sister Willodene, of course. Brother Hays is crumpled up on the mourners' bench. And there goes Nancy and Russ Bearden.

"Kneel in the pew, or whatever you do—"

"Want to be ready!"

"Get ahold of God! Get ahold of God!"

"Jee-sus!"

"Get ahold of God! Get ahold of the horns of the altar. Say: 'I'm not going to let go till I get an answer.' "

"Lord, Lord!"

"Find a place and pray. Everybody find a place of prayer. Find a place and call on the name of the Lord. Seek the Lord while He may be found! Call on Him while He is near!"

Then Brother Shad loosens his collar and spreads wide his arms. "Brothers and sisters!" he calls mournfully. "We wait but He will not tarry. We doubt but He will not fail. This is just the rehearsal, just the dressing room, for the real thing. For the time when the curtain really goes up. You better set your sights on elsewhere, on what you're dressing for–"

They're in for it now. It's a seesaw: they're up for the second, but here goes– Last chance tonight from Brother Shad as he says quietly, "We're right now living in the noon hour, the noon of opportunity, the last few hours–"

"After that–darkness–the night of gloom, the night of despair, the night of wrath. Men will be seeking and searching for a hiding place from the face of Him who sitteth on the throne!"

"Mercy, Lord!"

"Next Wednesday, Brother Wiggins is coming for a prophetic update–you be here! He's bringing tremendous powerful new evidence on the mark of the beast moving into our society. 666–the mark of the Antichrist! Also, the time of the gentiles, the ten federated nations, the Jew in prophecy, the Antichrist, the battle of Armageddon, and Lebanon at this very moment. You be here! Jesus is not saying that his coming is near, but at the door.

"The next step that God takes in prophecy is to transport his church. Flying over Plainview yesterday, I heard a voice from the control room: 'Even now preparations are being made in heaven to receive my bride.'

Didn't know whether I'd get to Lubbock or not before the Rapture took place. Yes, sir, it's gonna lift the roof—gonna lift the lid off Rooftree! You be there. Since yesterday I've been in a state of ex-treme anticipation. These are not ordinary days. These are the very last days, the very last moments trickling away. The excitement is mounting every minute—"

"All ri-ght!"

But now Sister Fry's got everybody's attention gathered to herself. She must of gone quietly down a side aisle when nobody was looking, for she's down flat on her back before the mourners' bench, slain under the Power, all of ninety-some years, slain in the Spirit, only her feeble arms moving, stroking the air a little.

And Brother Shad commends her, "You can't be proud and be a Pentecostal. You can't come to the Lord in a demanding spirit. You have to be nothing."

Now Sister Loretta is helping Sister Fry back to her feet, they've knocked over the budget pie and the easel it was on, Sister Fry kinda tottery, but she's still lifting those thin sticks of arms to praise the Lord.

"Lift up your head," Brother Shad calls to her. And then, spreading his hands, to all: "Redemption draweth nigh! The signs of the times are everywhere—men with unholy, unnatural affections, lovers of their own selves, covetous, boasters, proud, high-minded, blaspheming God. Sin is in! Evil men waxing worse and worse, treasuring up wrath. The half-hearted, the lukewarm, the savorless salt, shall be spewn forth—"

"I see a crimson stream of blood," Brother Hays is belting out.

And Henrietta and the high voices rush in–"Stream of blood!"

"It flows from Calvary."

"Calvary!"

"Its waves which reach the throne of God–"

"Throne of God!"

"Are sweeping over me."

"Over me!"

They sing on, with the high voices seconding, echoing, all the way to the finale, to "the portal where life forever reigns," but Brother Shad isn't resting with that, won't be resting until every last soul's gathered up there with him.

"Sin is in!" Brother Shad shouts. "The most agonized voice in hell is 'almost!' from the souls of men and women who were in reach of getting saved. In reach of the altar–"

"Oh, my God."

"Hey, this is the last generation! Because this generation and this world is going to its deathbed right now. When you're on your deathbed are you going to be watching R-rated movies on television?"

"No! Oh God!"

"How many of you if you were on your deathbed would be reading *Playboy* magazine? My friends, when you're on your deathbed, you're not thinking about no playbody, 'cause you're staring right into the eyeballs of the Judge. And you know that you've done wrong."

"Mercy, Lord–"

Brother Shad's cheeks look scalded, so hot. He takes out his big white handkerchief and buries his face in it. Time out–but Henrietta knows it's not for long. "I'm sick and tired of playing church!" he announces, mashing his handkerchief to a pulp and flinging it aside. "It's a lost and dying world out there. Whosoever's made a compromise with the world, a pact with the devil, a contract with Hollywood, I think it's time to sign a contract with Jesus Christ. I think it's contracted to have a date with the Lord of all eternity.

"I'm telling you He's gonna separate the chaff from the wheat. He's gonna separate the goats from the sheep. God's going to put you in his shaker in these last days." And Brother Shad falls to his knees. Folds his arms cross his chest, sort of cradles his own self in his arms, and rocks, and rocks. It sure isn't a lullaby. Henrietta slides to the edge of her seat, leaning hard forward but not kneeling, her head low, the rim of the pew biting her chin. She's hot, stiff, whipped with the day's labor. So tired. What she'd like most in all the world is a cool shower, the crash of cool tingling drops, drops a little blue with chill, they crowd out any other thoughts. Brother Shad is shivering, wailing, "He's not gonna be able to shake me out of the shaker!" and then she can't make out another blessed word, his teeth are clattering so loud.

He's calming now, though, a little, slowly rising to his feet, still swaying, but slower each swing, his face all sleeked with sweat. Softly, he speaks, "I want every head bowed, every eye closed. I'd like for any ladies that would like to come to kneel right over here, so that the ladies of the church can work with you. I want any men that want to come to kneel over on this side so that the men can work with you over here and pray for your soul's salvation. Will you come? As we sing the hymn of invitation.

While we stand together, while we sing. Are you ready? Will you come right now while the spirit of God is drawing. No more waiting–or debating. Saints of God, don't just stand there! Pray! Pray, saints! Close your eyes–get ahold of God! Pray that somebody will come. God bless this young lady. Go right down there. That's right. Everyone standing under the sound of my voice, this is the moment. Don't walk away saying no to the Lord tonight. Come now. While the Lord is knocking at your heart. Say yes to the Lord! Say yes to Him. Oh, yes, yes, yes, yes! *Multitudes, multitudes in the valley of decision . . .* Is there another young lady, a young man? Come on, right now. Are you ready for judgment day? You can get ready– come on, come on. God bless this young man. And you. Over here, good buddy. Right over here, on this side. That's right. Make room for him. God's gonna meet you, son. Bless you. Lost man, lost woman, won't you come? Praise God! Thank you, Jesus, thank you." It sounds like a multitude going down, but Henrietta's head is bowed, her eyes closed, she's not checking on Brother Shad. The one time she did, the devil must of prompted her, she peeked and all she saw was one poor lone soul, Brother Hays, crumpled up on the mourners' bench. Doubt, and that's what you get–more doubt–exactly what you deserve.

"Oh God, there's a hunger in her heart!" Brother Shad is wailing again. "There's a desire to seek you, Lord. Somebody else, somebody else . . . God bless this young lady! That's right. Is there any other young lady? Any other young man?

"Oh, that's right, pour out your heart to the Lord.

Sir, come on tonight. Sir, tonight is the night. God is calling you right now. It's a lost world, there isn't a moment to spare. Today is the day of salvation. Won't you come and kneel at this old-fashioned altar now? Now's your chance. Lost man, lost woman, won't you come? God bless this woman. Are you ready? Are you ready for judgment day?"

Somebody's weeping, somebody's laughing, voices crowd in from all sides, but things are winding down. "A church home, a burden lifted . . . ," the last call is going out.

"I Surrender All" is the last hymn. The very last altar call. Last chance, but Henrietta's still holding back. She isn't budging. Not tonight. Whatever she's done, she isn't sorry enough tonight. And she's surrendered enough. She knows the Lord will surely come. It'll be like a magnet passing over, and some of the nails are true iron and some not, and the true will fly up. Of course, she hopes to be among them. Who doesn't? She appreciates what Brother Shad is saying, but it's not biting into her like once it did when each and every word seemed aimed at the secretest, blackest chamber of her heart. She's heard this before, and —she's just not ready to quit the earth. It's too interesting now. And maybe she'll be surprised, maybe they'll all be surprised. She wonders how Sister Marcy's holding up all this long while, then recalls that Marcy disappeared early on, before the testifying. Must of stopped by only to show off the baby. She hopes Marcy's going to get a little time with the new baby here in Durance before they both get glorified bodies and go sailing off. But—why would

they want glorified bodies now? When even Henrietta—
tired, sweaty, itchy with the heat, with bunions on her
toes, wattled, addled, sagged and saddlebagged—doesn't
really want one. This body is all right, fits like an old boot.
She'll take what she knows. Brother Shad is calling out:

"Anybody else that wants God?"

Corpus Christi

A bad dream. He is in solemn procession, Bishop Fell, mysteriously, at once beside and behind him. The bishop's miter is pointed like an angry tooth, bicuspid, red silk between the white points. In one motion, they kneel before the tabernacle, Father Gilvary falling face forward, tripping over his own stole. He glances up, following the tilt of the bishop's miter. The tabernacle door is gaping. Inside: a loaf of bread, ordinary store-bought bread, still in its cellophane wrap.

Waking, his mouth is dry with fear. His hand passes lightly over his face, over his eyelids, heavy, still warm with dreaming. He's had this dream before, with and without the bishop. Strange . . . how the tabernacle dream, with its precisely contained fear, displaces the other fear—the shapeless one.

Going blind! Losing his nearest, dearest sense . . . He knows it is happening to him, but cannot take it in, doesn't quite believe in what he knows. He has heard. It was said to him. The losses he can register are gradual so far. Something happened yesterday, though—it puzzled, scared him a little. It was after his eight o'clock. On his way out, about to lock up, he was surprised by a stranger, a man in soiled overalls, sitting in a back pew. Someone he hadn't noticed before. When the man extended a hand toward him, he'd flinched—for the flash of a second, all he could see was a paddle shoved in his face—he hadn't recognized it as a hand. True, the hand had come at him from an odd, abrupt angle—

From the little Dr. Stas has said, Father Gilvary gathers that he's supposed to be thinking through his life to come, working out the logistics. But to practice blindness in advance seems as wrong to him as to extinguish a lagging, yet still beating heart. He wants, instead, to be fully present in this time.

Yet, hour by hour, he finds himself taking leave of things. Last night, it was the wedding photograph of his parents, scanning its age-browned surface with a magnifying glass, reading it like a close text, with a hunger for detail he has never known before. Noticing how lightly his father, a man of black and angry moods, rested his hand on his mother's shoulder. How he loomed over his bride, his head ever so slightly inclined, as if a word had just been whispered into his ear, a word he might have misheard.

It was, Father Gilvary supposed, one of the standard wedding compositions of the day: one seated, one standing, one dark-suited, one in white; the potted ferns, the imitation Oriental rug at their feet were, he imagined, the usual props. Meant to suggest luxury they were never to know.

Neither bride nor groom smiled. Her long fingers were ornamentally draped over the folds of her skirt, a dollop of lace on each wrist. The lace and the too-careful idleness were clearly unnatural, part of the pose for that one special day. They'd come from Aughavas in County Leitrim to find work in the new world, to Philadelphia first, then Chicago: he, as a steelworker; she, as a domestic. Backbreaking work; five children to come–all but himself, the youngest, gone now. From a marriage stormy at best.

Statues . . . had been Father Gilvary's first thought on picking up the photograph; they are placed in that moment for all time. And yet, on closer inspection–the look of perplexity in his father's face, the straining at distance in his mother's eyes, point to something still unsettled then, and now perhaps forever, unresolved. His mother seemed to be staring at a point far off, to the furthest apex of an intricate triangulation still in process. A place charted, promised. Not yet in view.

Impossible to fathom what it was she saw. Most likely, it was only the photographer, calling out, "Look here!", and pointing to his nose. She'd been nearsighted from childhood and never worn glasses. Nearly blind at the end–

Five after six! Nearly day. He tips the shade. Already

the sky is brass. God bring rain, everything cries for it. He spies the old woman across the street, moving crabwise down the path, dangling one long clawed arm in front of her. It takes a minute to make sense of the apparition: the long arm is one of those grocery clamping sticks used for reaching the high shelves, something new. So she can pick up the newspaper without stooping. Morning after morning, Father Gilvary has witnessed her laborious bending, her stiff arm inching.

And now she's close. Attagirl: she's hooked it. Never give in. *While it is day* . . . how does that go? *I must do the work of Him who sent me while it is day* . . . And the rest? Mmm. Father Gilvary's memory comes up short.

Manet una nox omnibus–one night awaits us all . . . No, he's mixing things. That text–Horace?–is not in his breviary.

Time to be up, and Father Gilvary is eager for it. Switching on the fan, he hears, or feels, the glass of the window shudder in response, something he's never noticed before.

Only four of the faithful at his eight o'clock. Before pronouncing the words of dismissal, Father Gilvary prays silently, *Lord, open our lips–our hearts.* He adds: *Hallow this time, this ordinary time. Make new our days as of old.*

He locks the church doors behind him on his way out. Nourished with heavenly manna, he thinks treacherously of coffee and cinnamon twist at Three Square Meals.

Old habits die hard, what it is . . . There used to be a crowd from Saint Jude's going that way; they'd gather for what Jim liked to call "a little post-Communion communion." The late Jim Traffis . . . Only rarely, these days, does Father Gilvary run into any of his parishioners at the restaurant; he could as easily have coffee and a doughnut at home. So why bother going there? He enjoys the bustle, that's part of it, the permission to sit and stare. Being in the midst: life flowing all around him. Now, more than ever, he appreciates the stir.

Place is crowded today. The new waiter—not so new anymore—could not be more efficient. He doesn't waste words and he seems never to slack off. Calls himself "Val." Nickname? Or what?

Today, Father Gilvary makes the mistake of trying to engage him in conversation, intending nothing more than a little social lubrication. An innocent-enough question, and Father Gilvary can't be the first to have asked it. Just: "What brings you out this way?" No answer, not a flicker of response. It's as if he hasn't heard the question, though Father Gilvary can tell by how carefully he sets down the check that it has registered. Something simply claps shut in Val. "I was running it through my mind," Father Gilvary explains. "Thinking out loud, that's all." But Val is already on his way to another table.

Prying, is what he must think. Or fishing for converts—what everybody thinks. Father Gilvary debates whether or not to stop by and see Jake in the hospital as he'd promised; then decides to risk it—because? There is no because. Risk it.

There's a new man in Jake's bed. "Gone," he says, "done gone and went!" Father Gilvary must look crestfallen, for he adds quickly: "Home, Father. He went home.

Left the day before yesterday. Said to make sure and thank you if you came by."

"You look surprised, Father."

"I am," says Father Gilvary, "happy for him."

"Went back to Oklahoma City—where his family's at. He said you visited with him about going back."

So.

The least little thing, sometimes.

Pete, too, has returned home. "In remission"—it's on his chart.

Much fortified, Father Gilvary decides to set out for the Warings' house; he's been meaning to do this for weeks. He hasn't driven but three or four times since his visit to Dr. Stas, only when there was no other way. Even before that time, he'd been cutting back, for it had been while driving that he'd had his first inkling that something was amiss with his vision. Times when all he could make out were the blank shapes of the traffic signs, the words obliterated. Even the shapes, with light eroding the borders, were none too distinct; he'd gotten in the habit of stopping at every corner to be on the safe side. He'd blamed it on the sun.

Been trimming back on other things, now that he thinks of it. Using the second eucharistic prayer day in and day out. True—it's his favorite. But it's also the briefest; he knows it by heart. He's been cutting down on his reading during liturgies wherever he can, having his deacon do the gospel. Trying to spare his eyes, for how long now? And not noticing? Or half-noticing—mentally glancing away? One small adjustment after another, nothing significant yet—when does the sum become active deception?

This visit isn't absolutely necessary, but he'd prefer not to delegate it. He owes it to Lee Waring to keep an eye on her house. Her will is to be probated in September. Father Gilvary doesn't expect any complications. No one to contest it: Jack and Lee were childless, and their kinfolk live back east in St. Louis.

Driving along in second ought to steady things. The roads are bound to be empty this time of morning, and Father Gilvary intends to go slowly. The route is second nature to him, ought to be, after all these years; the landmarks—two stoplights, grain elevator, railroad crossing—unmistakable. He eases out onto Farm-to-Market road.

Another brilliant day, everything starred, cracked—shattered—with light. *Light from light* . . . How strange that was, last Sunday. There, on his near right, stood a handful of the deaf, signing the Creed as they did every Sunday. Casey and Eula were leading, their performance perfectly routine.

And yet inexpressibly new. Losing the small gestures, his attention shifting to the broad, how extraordinary their dance of hands became! A clapping of wings on the word "heaven," and, at "light from light," their curled hands lifted and shattered, pods scattering spores of light.

In his homily last Sunday, he'd misspoken—and spoken truly. He said "unappareled" for "unparalleled." That's how things were for him on Sunday—unappareled. An unmasking, the cerements of things unbound.

There are four turnings after he passes the grain

elevator, three kinds of road—one blacktop, one caliche, one dirt. Starting up the third road, he hears another car fuming in his wake. Father Gilvary slows down while the pickup surges past him and dissolves in a spattering of dust.

Jack and Lee Waring . . . How time goes by.

Jack Waring had died during Father Gilvary's first year in Durance; they'd not had a chance to get to know one another well. A year or two after that, Lee had begun working at the church as a volunteer and, through the years, had become a real support to Father Gilvary. (And more, people rumored, but it wasn't so.) She'd had a hand in everything, though: Ladies' Altar Society, Legion of Mary, Anna Confraternity, taking Communion to the sick and shut-ins, helping out at Bingo and raffles. She'd slowed down last year, then passed away suddenly at the end of April, leaving the house and all the furniture to Saint Jude's.

You can't miss it; the house stands half-hidden in a clump of cottonwoods, the only trees for miles around. Father Gilvary mounts the porch steps, then pauses a moment at the door, as if to knock. Breathes *peace to this house*, and enters.

Inside, it's musty. Nothing seems to have been moved, but emptiness and silence have seeped through. The shades are drawn, the white walls look gray in the half light, everything shadowed—stained with neglect.

He stands on the threshold of the living room. Nothing has changed. It is a room Father Gilvary knows well. Years back, waiting for Jack to die, he sat in this room, moving from wing chair to sofa and back, hour after hour.

The sofa was too short to allow him to stretch out, so he'd napped in the wing chair. When he was unable to sleep or to concentrate on his breviary, he'd studied instead the things around him.

It is a room meant to be read: there's little in it that does not signify. Even the light switch covers are embossed with figures of Jesus quietly smiling, pointing to his exposed and burning heart. Bible on the coffee table, open to the text for Lee's next-to-last morning. Rosary in the ashtray, as she left it.

Nothing has been moved: the floral sofa, the two smaller armchairs stiffly flanking the sofa, the doilies, precisely centered, yellowing on their armrests. He stares at the big wing chair in the facing corner; his gaze rests on its deep hollow, shaped to the contours of an absence.

The house will have to be rented or placed on sale, the furniture sold. The extra income will be welcome at Saint Jude's, but will not save it. Funeral by funeral, Father Gilvary has been working himself out of a job.

He'll have to have the silver appraised, and the antique breakfront. Maybe call Fred Griffin about it.

Father Gilvary sits momentarily on the edge of the couch and silently mouths some words of prayer for Lee, *in your kindness sustain her in body and soul, where You live and reign,* but the words are weightless. He closes his eyes and murmurs, *Be seeing you,* and beholds a sea blur of hands waving. The words that well up are not from his prayer book, but those of a song his father used to sing. *May the road rise up to meet you . . .* They'd sung that song at Jack's wake.

No use lingering here.

Watch the road.

Four turnings, three kinds of road—dirt, caliche, blacktop. Father Gilvary slowly wends his way back, fingering the wooden rosary knotted on his gearshift as he goes. The joyful, the sorrowful, the glorious, that—he'd been promised—was the rhythm of things. But well short of the glorious, his mind wanders.

And soon he finds himself humming that old Irish tune, "May the wind be always at your back, may the sun . . ." They'd sung that at his father's wake, and again, not a month later, at Uncle Huey's. "Until we meet again . . ." The windshield clouds with tears.

He must be weaving badly—

The whirling lights, red and blue, are gaining on him now. Materialized out of thin air. No question he's the target.

"License, please."

Father Gilvary bends to the glove compartment.

"Sorry, Father," the officer pokes his head through the window, face close. "You were wobbling there."

Father Gilvary comes up with a fistful of documents —insurance, title deed, maps. There it is: the officer plucks it out.

"It'll be a warning ticket this time. Better concentrate on the road, Father. No use rushing the pearly gates before your time."

Father Gilvary stuffs the mess of papers, pink slip on top, into his glove compartment and drives slowly, ever so watchfully, home. No more singing. *Chained as I am to ten leopards* . . . The rosary beads dangle idly, swaying and chattering to themselves as Father Gilvary shifts gears, but there are no further mishaps.

Quick bite before his afternoon appointments. He has a marriage rehearsal coming up at one. Then Hannah Dunn with something that's been on her mind. (He's mentally slotted that for an hour.) Then—Confession.

He blesses himself before digging in.

The rehearsal is off to a bad start. No sooner does Father Gilvary step into the church when he finds the groom-to-be monkeying with the sanctuary lights. He once surprised an undertaker doing the same thing. It gets Father Gilvary's Irish temper up, now as before. "I don't go into your house," he raises his voice, "and mess with your lights."

But it is not his house.

They're all a little subdued after that, a little abashed, and seem to be hurrying through the rehearsal so as not to take up too much of his time. Now Father Gilvary has to work to slow them down. "Don't you want to show off your beautiful dresses?" he appeals to the maids of honor, as he lines up the bridesmaids and groomsmen with five pews between each couple. The rehearsal goes well, without the usual clowning around, and is over before the hour.

The next item on his agenda, though, is every bit as trying as expected. Hannah Dunn is leaving Saint Jude's for the big Christian Fellowship across town. Where the action is.

"Herb and I feel closer to God there," she says, her voice fluting.

Father Gilvary has nothing to say to that.

"It's your absentmindedness, Father." She pulls at the loose skin of her throat and frowns. "We want the gospel from you. Al Coglin is only a deacon—why do you have him always reading it? And why is it you never tell us how to save our souls? Preach the gospel, Father."

Really, there's no point arguing. He answers wearily, "I am preaching the gospel." And trying to live it, he thinks, best I can. "But go where you feel closer to God, Hannah. I won't stand in your way.

"I wish you well," he adds.

For a minute or two, they stare at one another in silence; they listen to the scratching of the overhead fan. It's a dare, thinks Father Gilvary, for his easy acceptance seems to have troubled Hannah more than anything he has said before. Now perhaps he has forced her hand. He simply hasn't the energy to play along. Precious little for anything else, and no surplus for games.

Then it all comes tumbling out, a treasury of grievances, stored up over who knows how long. "The Kemeny girls . . . receiving Holy Communion with gum in their mouths. Somehow you manage to continually overlook that, Father."

"I'll look into it, Hannah."

"That's what you said before. I've told you time after time. They have no respect for anything, those youngsters."

"I'll look into it."

"I think you should know there are others feeling like I do."

"I see," he says, closing his eyes.

Saturday at four is weekly Confession. "Sacrament of reconciliation," as they call it now, an opportunity for spiritual scrub-up before taking Communion. And not that much heeded these days. Post-conciliar Catholics seem to prefer talking things over with the priest in the office, face to face. They're as likely to confess to psychiatrists, bartenders or hairdressers. So Father Gilvary makes his way to the hot box, prepared for a long and lonely vigil. He spreads his ribbon stole across the small high table. There's a drawer in the table, gorged with books, that cannot be fully opened or shut. No point trying to unstick it now. Those were the days of luxury, the days of reading while he waited.

Now he simply waits. Silently, meticulously, he catalogues his fears: dropping the host; mistaking the page; failing to recognize the face, misreading the gesture, missing the point. Before long, he'll be stumbling in the house, cutting or burning himself. He lights the stove with special attentiveness now, but, one day, he's likely to forget.

Above all, he fears dropping the host. An occupational fear of young priests; most grow out of it–he did, but it is fully warranted now.

At four-twenty, two elderly women enter the church. The Bremen sisters: he knows by their timing and their tread. They arrive faithfully at twenty minutes after four every Saturday. Martha, the eldest, is first, making arthritic adjustments as she settles on the kneeler, the light over the grille wavering on and off.

They have, as usual, nothing to confess, nothing but their small meannesses to one another. Yet the chant goes on. It sounds as if Martha Bremen is ticking off a shopping list; for a second, Father Gilvary thinks he hears paper rustling.

Small sins, venial and natural under the circumstances. The Bremen sisters live alone together, ailing and aging in two small rooms.

How little is ever confessed . . . His own case a case in point. It's not that he hasn't tried, but his confessor Father Bill Dennehy is getting on, deafer every month; Father Gilvary has simply allowed himself to slip away in the beneficence of the older man's misunderstanding.

No, that wasn't quite it—deafness was only a part. To be more accurate, Father Gilvary contributed to that misunderstanding, speaking only of "worry, distractions, trouble with my eyes," and "the feeling that I've got to hold on, but I don't know why." With Bill answering in the kindest way, laughter in his voice: "What's this? Last minute doubts about your calling? Now?"

"Oh, hardly," he'd tried to answer with the same lightness. "There've been times of conviction, though. This isn't one of them. There've been times of fervor, of joy. I remember the first Mass I celebrated as a priest—my hands were shaking so. An old man called me 'Father.' Me! Young enough to be his son—grandson, maybe. I could have wept. When I lift the cup, even now, I still feel the same—the same presumption, same fear. Same joy—why do I forget that part of it? I've so many reasons to be grateful

. . . Lee Waring, Jim Traffis, Lorena, John, all the good people I've come to know! I have been so blessed."

"Say what? I'm sorry, I missed that. You say you're missing Jim? Still taking his death hard?"

"And Lee's."

"How's morale in the parish?"

"What would you expect? There've been so many deaths, one after the other. So much is ended."

"Debts?"

"Deaths. And, for me, doubts."

"It's the 'dark night' thing again?"

"Well, and then this other thing–"

"Now wait! This is important. Stick with this. Let's go over it again–what is it that happens when you pray?"

"When I try to pray, you mean"–he'd corrected Bill, admitting that it was an arid time–"the longest dry spell I can recall," that he worked at prayer, the right words came to him, but his mind wandered. The effort was grinding, really.

"God doesn't demand perfect concentration, as you well know–only surrender."

"Only!"

"Just–sell everything."

"It's pretty much all been sold, you know, by now. And not entirely by my own doing."

"That's the nub–surrender. You're clutching again. Trying to control what can't be controlled. It's the old story–you see these things in others, but you fail to apply them to yourself. Open your hands, Tom. Quit clutching." And, with that, they'd embarked on a discussion of the prayer most meaningful to him. The Anima Christi, Father Gilvary supposed.

"What draws you to that one?"

"Hard to say. But it does draw me." What was it? The utter nakedness of need in it, he thought. The ending was a bit of a wheedle, though.

"Say it—out loud—once a day," Bill advised. "Say it, listen to yourself saying it. And then—listen!"

After driving to the Eye Clinic in Letsem City only to have confirmed what Dr. Stas had told him, he had pushed on to Bill's parish in Castaño to make his confession. Both he and Bill might be called "professionals" at this, yet, somehow, between them, the heart of the matter, this business of impending blindness, had managed to slip away . . .

Only a few more minutes to wait in the confessional. Feeling a little claustrophobic, Father Gilvary shuts his eyes. The too-close walls dissolve. With the fevered clarity of dream sight and large as life, he sees Bishop Fell settling on the kneeler, poking his head through the space where the grille should be, as though it were a post office window. The bishop says not a word but, with elaborate casualness, slips off his episcopal ring and sets it down on the narrow ledge between them. Now he is rubbing his ring finger, as if to relieve a constriction. It's a familiar ploy; he pulls the ring routine whenever he means to speak to you in his humanity.

Another in the bishop's repertoire is the informal visit, casual to the point of taking off his shoes (a thing unthinkable in pre-conciliar days). Getting cozy in the stagy way politicians do, propping his stocking feet up on

the coffee table. And talking of "team players," "team spirit."

The problem is that Father Gilvary thinks of the "team" as the parish, while Bishop Fell means chancery, or the priest-senate sort of thing, some sort of occupational clubbery.

Father Gilvary opens his eyes. Bishop Fell is much, too much, on his mind. It's no mystery why. Soon he'll have to make an appointment with the bishop. They'll discuss the terms of Father Gilvary's retirement, and the future of Saint Jude's; it must be done.

Soon, but not yet: Father Gilvary is not yet ready. He must pray for Bishop Fell. He mouths a single word of invocation: *Lord*– Nothing further comes. It's the heat– suffocating. Time to close up shop. He's not about to spend a minute more in the box.

Tonight he eats at the cafeteria on Line Street, the big one with so many booths that no one knows he's there.

Back home, still in light. The days are long now. He's weary–bone weary. Wherever his gaze rests there is glare and after-image, as if he'd been staring too long at the sun.

It's been dry so long, and there's no relief in sight. Father Gilvary's glad to be inside, but where can he settle? He decides on the chair by the open window in the bedroom–an ancient rectory chair, high and rigid, with carved wooden armrests, curled talons at their ends. There's another armchair in the room, a recliner that's ever so much more comfortable, but too difficult to clamber in and out of, having locked in the highest feet-up position. Too much bother to bring in anyone to fix it, too expensive to buy another.

He gazes out the open window. Over the lawns, the sprinklers are whirling. You can fairly hear the grass rustling, drinking, thanking, it's so parched.

Father Gilvary is determined to pray and, since prayer can happen anywhere, tries just where he is in the claw-handed chair. But now some boys have started up a game of Frisbee in the middle of the street and the commotion crowds out his thoughts.

Very well, he'll turn his chair to face the wall. Soon as he does, though, the sight of his silver jubilee award—the number "25" mapped out in quarters, glued to black velvet—distracts him. The Sisters of Perpetual Adoration presented him with this years back. The quarters gleam: six dollars, all told. Even to let his gaze rest on them for half a minute starts a jingling in his ears.

He wants desperately to pray. He thinks of Father Harkins, the earliest priest he can remember, recalling the man's dandruff, his stale breath in the confessional. Father Harkins talked about "knitting" (there were a lot of jokes about that), about prayer knitted into your life, your life knitted into divine life through prayer.

But it's all loose, nothing's linking here.

Finally, Father Gilvary decides to use the church. It's bound to be hot inside, but not as close as the confessional.

It's dim in the sanctuary, dim in the nave, but he knows every step of the way by heart. The only light is from the ruddy sanctuary lamp and the pale, flickering tongues of the votive candles. Father Gilvary settles in his favorite pew, facing the tabernacle. The bleary red eye of the sanctuary lamp greets him. He turns to it.

O bone Jesu, exaudi me . . . A breath passes over his face, touches his eyes, a moth the color of smoke. *Hear me—*

Hrspp . . . A candle lisps in a breeze. The place is a whispering gallery. Which window did he forget to close?

He wonders whether tomorrow's Mass schedule was properly posted in the parish bulletin.

Now—where was he?

He'd been trying to pray, and failing. The darkness seems steeper now, though only minutes have passed since entering the church. *O good Jesu, hear me* . . . The words come easily, but shadows clutch at his heart.

Within thy wounds hide me;
Suffer me not to be separated from Thee . . .

He speaks his intentions afterward. For the quick and the dead, blood kin and parish family—even, by a stretch of magnanimity, throwing in Bishop Fell while he's at it. At once, the prayerful spell is broken. He tries again, invoking the name of Father John Kenny, still at death's door at his sister's home in Lawton—*Grant him a peaceful passage to the eternal kingdom*—but when Father Gilvary realizes that these are the very words of the mimeographed memo from the chancery, he breaks off.

Time for bed. He stands in the open door of the rectory for a moment before locking up for the night.

Hot and dusty still.

Lights are burning in the hallway; he switches them off as he goes. Strange . . . how the lights don't die out right away, but linger with trailing threads. How tangled those threads are in all the furniture of the world. He'd never noticed before.

A dry season. He's steadily losing at prayer, he knows, losing the concentration, if not the conviction. Yet, if nothing else, he reflects, his rituals of opening up and closing, of sweeping the church steps free of leaves and snow in season, are prayerful. Are prayers in their way.

Or are they just compulsions—rafts to which he clings in the drifts of time?

Father Gilvary is fumbling with his microphone again. It's one of those clip-on devices, no bigger than an olive. A triumph of technology, no doubt, but it never stays clipped, so he holds it delicately, like a rosebud, half an inch from his nose. His words are mixed with the sounds of nasal breathing and the nervous scratching of his thumb.

In his youth, back in Chicago, the feast of Corpus Christi—*festum sanctissimi Corporis Christi*—had been a day of solemn procession, Father Gilvary recalls. The Blessed Sacrament was borne aloft in a beautiful heart-shaped monstrance, under a canopy supported by four of the faithful, "four living pillars of the parish," and followed by crowds that stretched for blocks. After the crossbearer came the flower girls, leaving a trail of petals in their wake, then an acolyte turning backward to incense the Blessed Sacrament. Three times they would pause at homemade altars to adore the Body of Christ.

Such processions were held less and less often in

these post-conciliar days, Father Gilvary observes, and something was clearly lost in their passing. Yet perhaps it would not be unfair to say that something was also gained. For the feast of Corpus Christi, now stripped of its spectacle, had become a Holy Thursday for ordinary time, a day of reflection on the meaning of the Body of Christ, on the working of Christ in the world.

"We are his wheat. We are the grains scattered, threshed, and gathered . . ." And now Father Gilvary has his theme well in hand. "Christ at the table of the human family is the one food and drink which changes the eater into the eaten. We are to be the Body of Christ, to become bread for others, the broken bread—"

A heavy lethargy in the congregation this morning as he speaks of the five loaves and two fishes shared out among multitudes. "So the smallest gifts placed in trust in the Lord's hands can still multiply to work wonders today as they did in Galilee long ago." Someone coughs, another takes it up. They all look half asleep. There will be no multiplication of wonders today. As he moves away from the lectern, Father Gilvary can hear the front row sighing with relief.

Once the collection is taken, Father Gilvary positions himself in front of the altar, where he will stand to welcome the bearers of the offering. He opens his hands to receive the bread, the water and the wine.

No one stirs, although heads turn. Bill Warren holds the collection basket chest high—he's ready. Who else was scheduled for today?

It must have been the Dunns, Hannah and Herb. This, then, is their revenge . . . Still, Father Gilvary waits, his arms stretched forth. Finally, much aggrieved, he speaks–words not in the liturgy: "I can do without the collection. But I cannot do without the bread–the bread!–the water and the wine."

The Bremen sisters are the first to oblige. Slowly, with eyes downcast, they bring the gifts forward.

Father Gilvary's hands are trembling. "Blessed are You, Lord, God of all creation," he begins the offertory. "Through your goodness we have this bread to offer, which earth has given and human hands have made . . ." How extraordinary–how perilous–that moment of waiting was! God waiting for us to be given back to himself, to be given to one another.

"It will become for us the bread of life."

Tumbleweed

"Cleat? That boy that's always hanging around? Name's Cletus. C-l-e-t-u-s. Sound like some kind of flower? Does to me. I never heard it before, either, but that's what they found pinned to the blanket he was wrapped in. Dropped out of nothing. They found him on the post office steps—like a letter somebody'd been trying to toss in the box, but missed." Henrietta punches out change. The customer drops it into his pocket without bothering to count. "Buck and Betty Miller—that's our postmaster, Betty's his wife—they took him in."

"Seen this?" He holds out a dab of paper too small

for folding. "Thought it might be one of those lost cat notices, why I took it."

Henrietta sighs, does not reach for the paper. She knows what it will be. It might be another, or it might be the same—they're all pretty much the same and she doesn't need to put on her reading glasses to find out. "I seen most all of them, I guess," she says.

"Thinks he's Jesus Christ Almighty."

"Now I doubt that."

"What church does he belong to?"

Henrietta is about to explain, but she's not real sure, herself. Buck and Betty are Baptists, of course, and Cleat started out that way—

"See, that's what I mean. He's free-lance—on his own. A church of one. Thinks he's Jesus Christ on the loose."

"There isn't an ounce of harm in him," Henrietta is quick to reply. "He's just sort of—" What is the word she wants? "Floaty. Know what I mean? Preacher here called him 'the work of a single night,' did I mention that? He's not well rooted. How could he?"

"As the twig is bent so the bough is sharpened," the man is Scripture-solemn as he says this. "He's spooked, no question."

"Creepy" is the word Stella uses. It's the same feeling.

Cleat was always a hanger-outer, as Henrietta recalls, but he never spent so much time at her place before. She knows what's drawing him.

Henrietta remembers him when he was just a button, a little bitty thing with carroty hair, bunch of freckles, and, even back then, eyeglasses. Kids used to call him

Tumbleweed

"Lem" for saying "Lemme" all the time, always wanting to tag along. Then he sprouted up and spun loose like tumbleweed. Like tumbleweed, he'd turn somersaults to hitch onto anything, anything that happened to blow by.

Couple years ago he started hanging out by himself. Didn't seem to need anybody. When Henrietta went by the post office, she'd spot him standing somewheres up or down the street, standing and strumming his air guitar. He'd gotten so spacey even the kids left off teasing him, and when he quit school and moved out of Buck and Betty's and into the YMCA nobody asked why or tried to hold him back. Most everybody thought that was only the first step, that he'd soon be on his way out of town.

But he hadn't budged from Durance, and it didn't look like he was about to. He was always around. And he worked. You could say that for him. Worked his butt off. You'd see him coming back from the graveyard shift at the post office, delivering flags on Memorial Day, doing yard work, mowing cemetery grass, selling salvage—whatever came along. And always, always handing out those notices. Hard to say if anybody read them. Nobody paid them much mind if they did.

Creepy . . . Going into Saint Jude's at night is like entering a deep forest. It's the gloom, the trees closing in on all sides, the noise of the wind slatting through wood.

Down front, in a pew that faces the hanging red lamp, he finds the priest. He's stooped over, praying. Or maybe sleeping? Cleat's never seen anyone sleeping as quiet as this. His eyes are closed, chin tucked under, almost touching his chest. Doesn't seem to be breathing, he's so still.

Cleat is pretty sure he was supposed to come in at eight to change the high light bulbs, and it's already seven after eight. He doesn't know where the bulbs are stored, or whether the tall ladder is still lying on its side against the wall in the basement. The way to the back of the church is through that skinny side door—behind it, the golden cup is kept—but he's not going to poke around without permission. He's heard that Catholic churches have secret cellars stuffed with treasure, and in Rome there's a whole palace full.

Maybe go back out, slam the door and come in again?

No, better wait. If Father Gilvary is dozing, it won't be long. Cleat chooses one of the back pews and stretches out to his full length. If only he could forget how spooky it is, he could easily nap right here on this bench. He hasn't slept much the past four nights, and last night—not at all. Something strange happened when he closed his eyes: he felt a membrane under the lids folding away, some wrapping, clear as a skin of water, invisible to the open eye; his eyelids fell shut and a curtain lifted. He wasn't dreaming, for he wasn't asleep, but it wasn't like being awake. What he saw was: pictures, moving pictures in his mind. He saw Val, his back turned, walking up the road, this long, steep slash of road, walking slow at first, then fast and faster.

Another strange thing: the farther Val went, the louder the sound of his footsteps. He moved to the beat of Cleat's own heart. Yet Cleat was powerless to slow him down. Cleat called out Val's name again, and again, the word blew out of his mouth and came back to Cleat, and Val hurried on, not once glancing back.

If only he would slow down and listen! Val didn't have to be alone. If he would listen. If he would stop for a second. Cleat hollered, trying to tell him that; Val kept on fleeing, growing smaller; Cleat followed, breathless, straining to keep the last speck of him in sight. And, all the while, Cleat knew that none of this was real. He was lying in bed, his eyes were closed. His heart was thundering, but it was only a movie of his mind.

Now he's stretched out on a pew at Saint Jude's, waiting for Father Gilvary to wake. Cleat's eyes are wide open. He's not seeing anything that's not here.

It's so quiet he can hear birds shifting from foot to foot on the roof. And something else. Wind, probably, this low, glassy moan like the wind makes over the mouth of an open jar. Just the wind—

But he's not sure.

The light in the church is queer, he notices, the dark not steady, but pulsing, like puffs and spackles. There are six rows of candles behind him. Only one is lit, a small pale smudge. The light blooms out, a little ways, then folds.

Something tap-tapping. That's funny . . . Cleat lifts his head to listen, then bolts upright. There is something! Somebody running? Somebody knocking? It's coming fast.

And now?

Nothing now. He swings his feet to the ground. The place is spooked. Priest looks like one of his statues.

Wait.

There it goes again. Loud. Sounds like metal on metal, the chonk and rattle of tow chains. Why doesn't Father Gilvary rouse to it?

Something topples–

Cleat is on his feet, calling out, racing for the door, heaving through it–

Have to be dead not to hear that!

He's running–past doors of houses all shut, all blind, there's a phone booth somewhere, couple blocks down. *Hey, hey–hey!* Who said that? He hears a commotion, a laughter of feet, close behind him, but glancing back sees only the empty street. Nobody. Only the commotion of his own heart–

Booth isn't where he thought it was. He shouldn't of left–he should call the police right now. And he will, he will. Soon as he finds that phone–

He needs Val. Val will know what to do, together they'll do something.

At Henrietta's Restaurant, the phone's tied up. And Val's not around. "It's his night off," Henrietta tells Cleat. "No saying where he might be." She gives him Val's home address, then asks, "You all right? My goodness, what's the big hurry?" Cleat shakes his head: can't explain, no time. Starts off in a burst of speed, then gets such a stitch in his side that he has to freeze in place. *Wait*—he tells himself—be faster if you do. He knows he ought to head back to Saint Jude's.

The stitch is widening. Between his ribs, like a knife crack. Will nothing–nothing?–make his heart go slow? He stands, doubled over, arms pressed to his sides, waiting.

The stitch will pass, he knows, it always does. Always. So: breathe, look out, wait.

The shops are closed, some lighted, some dark. Streetlights coming on. He can see birds in the offing; they look like commas, so long gone.

The sky is so deep he's near swallowed in it . . .

He has to find Val. Val will know what to do.

He's nearly a block away when he first catches sight of the yellow house, but he recognizes it at once. He's done up the yard there, many a time. No one's sitting out on the porch tonight, it's too hot. He's running hard now, coming close, and up the porch steps, he's calling Val's name—then stumbling, missing the top one, is thrown to his knees. Wants nothing more than to stretch out, full length, and graze his face against the boards.

No, you don't. No time for it, and he's up again, knocking and calling. Then he notices the bell and rings. Presses the bell again, and again, his heart still climbing. No answer. Nobody around to ask.

What now? There aren't a whole lot of places to be in Durance. There's Kate's Feed and Spirits, the Keyhole Lounge. Maybe Fong's Golden Skillet— Val probably likes Chinese food, coming from the city and all. The Chinese are a really subtle people. Val would appreciate that.

Cleat heads for downtown.

"For years, I lived on sandy soil—I didn't know about black soil, how, if you stick with it when it's dry, it'll stick to you when it's wet. Put a foot in and a yard follows."

Black soil, sandy soil—Val could care less. He counts to himself, then hums, tunelessly.

Chump doesn't know how to take a hint.

His name's Leroy and he hangs around the laundromat most evenings. Wears a big hat with a fancy crease and a four-inch smiling brim. "You're bound to run into Leroy," Henrietta warned him weeks back when he asked where the laundromat was in town. "That's his idea of entertainment. He'll run through a pair of socks, or the shirt he washed out the night before. Gives out advice on the machines, plenty of it. He's retired, you see what I'm saying? It gives him something to do."

Getting dark out there. The shops up and down the street are shut. For all one knows, Val muses, this laundromat with its glaring fluorescent lights and rumbling dryers might be the only pocket of the living left on earth.

Val's concluded that Leroy is talking against the coming of night. He picks up speed the darker it gets. "Lived in a little town, name of Slocum," he says. He scoots an empty clothes basket over to the side and follows Val from the dryer to the folding table. "Ever hear of it?"

"Of what?"

"Slocum—this town I lived in."

Val shakes his head. He's trying to match socks.

"You wouldn't of. It's just a little speck in the mud."

"That's why you know so much about laundromats, I guess," Val says, "being stuck in the mud," and snorts at his own joke.

Leroy laughs right along with him. Then, abruptly,

sobers. Something catches their attention: a nose flattened to the glass. Red face staring in.

Inside, Cleat hunches over. His mouth is working without much sound coming out.

"You related?" asks Leroy, glancing from Val to Cleat. Val doesn't bother to answer, the question is so dumb.

"Are you all right?" Leroy turns to Cleat.

Cleat holds his arms clenched to his sides. He's having some trouble getting his wind back. His face is flushed, shiny with sweat, and his eyes are fixed on Val.

Val doesn't even look at him. "You're as hard to kill as a tin can," he says quietly.

Cleat breathes, "The priest that comes in–Father Gilvary–"

"Please?" says Leroy.

"He might be dead!"

"That so?" says Val.

"There's a phone out in back," Leroy is fishing in his pocket. "Number is 1-2-3. Here–I've got change. Call now."

But all Cleat does is stand there. Like he's nailed to the spot.

"I'll call for you if you tell me what it is," Leroy persists. "I'd want someone to do for me, you see, if I was in his shoes."

So Cleat turns to Leroy and tells him.

It was nothing, of course. Could of been wind, or the noise of birds–or maybe a kid–on the roof. On a dare or something. Kids do it all the time; the roof is flat, it's easy to clamber up there. It was Cleat with his air guitar all over again, spinning out tunes that nobody else hears.

Leroy phoned the police first, then the church, holding on till he got an answer. Father Gilvary had been napping is what it amounted to: he'd started out praying, and ended up in a doze. And that, Leroy explains to Henrietta, just goes to back up what he's always said. None of those preachers ever do a lick of work, except on Sundays and Wednesday nights, when they rattle the collection cans. Leroy has no use for preachers of any kind. Only reason he's gone to First Baptist for so long is on account of the singing, and the nicest he'll say of the pastor there is: "Brother Steptoe don't have a whole lot to say, but he sure takes a good long time to say it."

Henrietta doesn't pay Leroy too much mind when he gets on this subject. She knows his heart's in the right place. Leroy's the kind that's always saying, "No, I won't," and then goes and does. The Lord sees that. Has to.

Talking it over, Henrietta and Leroy both agree that Val isn't good for Cleat, but neither can think of what to do to stop Cleat from hanging around him. He'll have to grow out of it. You can't argue the boy out of it. Can't force him to see how hopeless and foolish it looks to anybody else looking on. Who could tell Henrietta such a thing when she's tumbling headlong, her heart leading? Who knew better than she?

Dolls

Henrietta leaves Sue and Frank Helm's anniversary party early, awash in loneliness. It was their thirty-fifth and it hurt so sore that she had to plead a headache and go.

She is glad to be home. Alone and lonesome is better than together and lonesome any night of the week. That's something she learned years ago, but keeps on forgetting. Last Saturday night, in fact. Saturday, it got so bad that she went and took Leroy home with her. He was always dawdling into closing time, smiling his mournful smile, so she invited him. He's nothing much to look on, but he is big, clean and polite–and male.

"Ma'am?" he said when she asked him, as if he hadn't heard her aright.

And she did get him to set beside her on the love seat in a kind of heavy cuddle. But all he really wanted to do was talk. "It's real nice here," he said, "I like things nice." He was real glad to come over, he wanted her to know that. So good to sit in a real home. " 'Preciate it," he said. For years now, he'd lived in a trailer, he'd fixed it up as best as he knew how. But, say what you would, a single fellow could not make a house a home.

What he talked about most was how hard his life had been. "Got dried out farming," he recalled. "For years I lived on sandy soil. Then I moved to Slocum–that's black soil–and got washed out. Worked for General Mills six, seven years as a feed packer. Sewed all them sacks of feed by hand. Drove a propane truck for another couple years, can't remember how long . . . Worked in a carbon black plant after that."

He'd been a strong one, Henrietta liked that.

"Good pay, and I've got smarts enough to know how to handle money. Suzy–that's my wife–passed on in '82. We had six kids–they're all growed now. Four girls, two boys, but they don't know what work is. We was fighting to survive back in those days . . ."

Henrietta wanted a man to lean on, she was tired of being a strong one. She laid her head on his shoulder, sighed with a windy gust, and sort of wilted in his direction, hinting. Didn't do a bit of good. When he asked her whether he hadn't better get a move on, she protested, "The evening's still a pup. Stay, why not stay?" So he did, he sat on for hours, hat in his lap, hands on his hat, talking.

That hat never traveled an inch till he shook himself out to go. There just wasn't any chemistry between them.

At least she has Terri, Kianne, Lucy and Kate. Henrietta decides to put Kianne into her nightgown and take her to bed. If she'd of had kids, she'd of known what to do. Every boy would have a dog, every girl a cat.

The baby she had with Charlie–that would of been the real Kianne–is nothing but a dream now. A dream that's always the exact same moment. In the dream, Henrietta is holding a rabbit that's hurt and blue with cold, this funny little rabbit with damp nose, no fur, and slick, crumpled skin.

Now this Kianne, with yellow wool hair, button eyes and a button nose, is real cute, soft and cuddly. And no messes, there's that to be said for her. But no heartbeat, either, and her eyes don't follow.

Henrietta tucks her in. "Night, love. Join you in a little," then heads for the kitchen. She's starved again. Not really starved, of course, just mooching around empty.

Nothing but nibbles left.

If she's going to eat anything it should be a carrot or a stick of celery. Or an apple–though she craves something sweeter. She knows exactly what it will be, has known all along; one of those chocolate doughnuts she hid from herself back of the lowest shelf in the refrigerator. She's been size 18 for the past year now, and holding, but one of these days she'll let herself go again. Get so fat she'll have to take a sheet, cut a hole in it for her head, and wear that. Chocolate, all by itself, will do her in.

One chocolate doughnut, then another, they simply melt in her mouth. She doesn't really taste them till they're sliding down the hatch, already turning to slather and regret. Licking the creamy glaze off her fingertips, Henrietta wonders at this. It's like she blinks when whatever it is she's longed for actually comes. Like she's holding her breath–harking back or dreaming ahead–almost missing the moment when it crests.

Oh, but she's had times . . .

Charlie liked her big– "The more of you, the better," bragging about it–but he was the only one. Drove up with a backhoe for their first date: "Come to give you a lift," he said. It's his sense of humor Henrietta misses most, like his ripply signature, not a bit like anybody else's.

Brushing the particles off her chest, she spies grit and crumbs everywhere. Now's as good a time as any, so she reaches for Dusty, her little hand vacuum, and starts mowing the table, the chairs, under the chairs, the kitchen counter.

When she's done with Dusty, she damps a cloth and starts to polish the knickknacks on the high shelf. She moves the cloth with special care over the spotted china dog. There's a notch in his ear. That happened after Charlie's time, in those months when R.D. was living with her, pickling himself in corn whiskey and raising all blistering hell. Accused her of sleeping around, was the occasion of it. She glued the ear back on but you can still see the seam.

She shines up the black china cat and the gray china squirrel chased by the cat. Can't think of anything to do now but to see what might be on television. Henrietta switches rapidly from channel to channel, but nothing interests her for long. At channel six, she holds: the Cadillac contest in Monroe has been going on for a week now. She's surprised to see so many still at it. Whoever keeps hands on the Cadillac longest owns it, that's the deal. They're allowed a ten-minute break for every hour of hands-on.

There's still a crowd of hands swarming over the car. Henrietta knows who's going to win. It's not the boy laying down with his legs under it, two fingers glued to the front wheel. It's that bald-headed fellow sitting on a folding stool, side by side with the car, the one that's chewing his cud; he's not even looking at the Cadillac. He shoots a quick jet of tobacco juice, low, off to one side. The camera catches the spurt, freezes it, holds it from frame to frame like something precious, a band of dark-spun, gleaming gold. That man hates the car with a passion, Henrietta can tell. It's one of those things she knows.

Henrietta hasn't had all that much schooling, but she knows a whole lot. Like how to train fleas—not many people know. When she told Brother Shad about that, he flowered it up and made his whole Sunday lesson out of it. But it was Henrietta that told him.

How you train fleas is you put them in a quart jar and screw down the lid. Fleas like to jump, so, soon as the lid's screwed down, they start getting headaches. Brother Shad called it "migraine headache number 55—Excedrin headache number 311." After a while they jump a little lower. Then you lift the lid, and they jump just high enough to miss the lid. Like us—we jump, we get whomped on the head, and we learn to jump only so high. "Can't do it," we say, "just can't."

Henrietta knows that nothing is impossible if you

but believe it. Even when she forgets, she knows. It's like Peter calling out to Jesus walking on the water: "That you? Bid me come." Nobody else in the boat asked. Only Peter dared to step out upon the water, and the little waves crowded in, saying, "Walk, walk, trust me, trust me," but when he looked down, when he took his eyes off the goal—that was Jesus—the waves were so boisterous that he feared. He feared and he doubted, though he knew—

And Henrietta knows. She knows that the hard times will pass, that every tear will be gathered, every word, spoken and unspoken, every sigh, each and every hair, feather, crumb that falls—every last particle will be counted and accounted for. The Lord's going to minister to every need. Nobody on earth knows what those needs are. But He knows.

It's so quiet she can hear the refrigerator humming. And plates, left to themselves in the drying rack, clank softly against one another. Or maybe a breeze starts them.

The Lord hears that, too. She believes it, just really does. Not that she hasn't been hooked and suckered into things aplenty. Even by men of God. That's because they were men, only human, not God. That they were up there praising the Lord didn't mean a thing, not a thing. Like that visiting evangelist years back, the one that called himself "Brother Peck." Henrietta was all tore up over Charlie, she loved him so bad, she was near to suicide with all of it. And then she'd taken up with R.D., and R.D. had walked out on her, and this Brother Peck said clear out of the blue: "Give it up! Put it into the Lord's hands," and his eyes were fixed on Henrietta. "There's a lady here whose husband's passed on, and friends have left her and she's thinking of suicide, but if she'll give twenty-seven dollars to the Lord she'll be all right." When Henrietta peeked in her purse, there it was—twenty-seven dollars was just what she had—so she gave all of it over in one whack. And felt better then, she did feel better. So even when Brother Peck disappeared with a bushel of bills, maybe she hadn't been snookered after all.

That was after Henrietta stopped going to Trinity Methodist. Too many memories of Charlie and herself together in church there, how she'd be in the choir loft and Charlie down in the pew, and there'd be an altar call and whoever got to the altar first would kneel down and save a place for the other alongside.

She couldn't go over to the big Christian Fellowship on North Goodvine because it put her in mind of the time she'd taken Charlie for a healing service with that visiting preacher from Arkansas whose name she never can remember. Things were going from bad to worse by then, Charlie had nothing to lose, but he'd refused to walk down the aisle and let himself be anointed. That night the preacher had cured three lame ones, two deaf, one mute, one with water on the brain, and his hand was pointing at Charlie, all red and trembly and swole with the ache to heal him. "There's a man here whose heart is missing every third beat," he declared. You couldn't miss where he was pointing. But Charlie dug in his heels, saying something curt and low he buttoned back under his lip, and wouldn't budge.

After Charlie, Henrietta went to the Baptists instead —the church over on Line Street. *A new start,* she told herself, though it wasn't all that different from Trinity Methodist. The other Baptists called the Line Streeters "wet Methodists." Too much love of God and not enough wrath of God to be true Baptists was what they said.

If Henrietta felt lonely with the Line Street Baptists it surely was of her own choosing. Everyone was extra friendly there. But she couldn't bring herself to fill out the name card, couldn't bear the thought of a home visitation, and, one day, a man turned to her and asked why she kept coming if she wasn't thinking of joining—was she looking for a husband?

She'd gone to the Pentecostals after that—Seven Lampstands, and, finally, Rooftree. When she had herself rebaptized—full immersion, no sprinkling—she enjoyed it so much that she started splashing everything around her. And after that she'd had her baptism of the Holy Spirit with a rushing wind and tongues of flame. Henrietta had long been a Pentecostal at heart, but hadn't known it until one night she bust out speaking in tongues. It sounded like birds talking and she could not believe the sounds were coming from her own mouth. It only happened once, but it was enough for Rooftree, a true baptism of the Holy Ghost. Right afterward, Henrietta had her doubts whether it'd been a real language she'd been speaking, but Sister Willodene set her straight on that. Sister Willodene said she'd read a book once about prisoners in England who'd been jailed for debt. It was in the olden days, one of those centuries. When the government couldn't afford to keep them anymore, the prisoners were set free and their tongues were split down the middle so they couldn't work again; that was their punishment, they could only beg. And guess what they sounded like?

Like birds talking!

So Henrietta knew she'd found her church home at last. That didn't mean that if she died tonight she'd go to heaven for sure; she was no fool. Yes, she was a sinner, many a time backslidden, yes, she needed to lay her burden down, needed a clean heart, needed to rededicate her heart to Jesus. Yes, oh my, yes, she invited Him in. Unceasingly.

For a couple of weeks before she found Rooftree, back in that bad time between Line Street Baptist and Seven Lampstands, she'd even tried the Romans where Father Gilvary was pastor, that's how bad off she was. Lord knows, the church was pretty enough, smelled nice, and the priest's robes were pretty. And the painted windows—that was another thing she liked. And how every time the priest's hand moved it said something. But it didn't ease her heart any, being there. The chilly bells, the old women mumbling and buttoning themselves up with little crosses, the curtsies, the chants, the calm of it, made her feel dozy, like smoke. She stood and sat when they did and, once, even went down on the kneeler. But it wasn't any use. She wasn't a member, didn't feel at home there, and knew she never would. Too little fever, too long a password, too many rules. She told herself that it was all self-feeding, a club.

Then she wondered how Rooftree might look to somebody coming in.

She'd been told, many a time, how the priest was nothing but an old man with a bag of tricks. How he was

in the grip of Satan–all Catholics were. They were prisoners of Rome, everybody knew that. Though she never
would believe that they worshipped statues, like Brother
Shad said they did.

And she wondered about the priest. You had to wonder about them not marrying and what they did with
themselves when they were young, how they got through
the nights.

Yet, still–still, Henrietta has a suspicion that the
Lord's house is even bigger than Brother Shad thinks it is.
It would take a heap of space, of course, it would have to
be a mighty big house to make room for Father Gilvary
and Brother Shad both, but nothing is impossible with the
Lord.

Henrietta wouldn't put it past Him.

Falling Weather

Rain is on everyone's mind. Dreaming rain, talking rain, remembering rains gone by. "After this country gets some rain, I think you can just feel it respond," Henrietta hears one of the old-timers explaining to Val. Val is staring back at him with one of his I-can't-believe-what-I'm-hearing expressions, his eyebrows raised, and he doesn't blink at all. Not once. "When it rains I either want to go out and drive around in it," the old man rambles on, "or set out on the porch and watch it and listen to it. It's somewhat of an event. We never get much, but I can't ever remember it being dry so long."

They talk about rain more than they talk about the

June fair, more than the man who eats snakes or the smallest horse in the world, or the two-headed pig, or the sheep with six legs. They call the dust "West Texas gold," and joke how it will be the only gold coming their way this season. When they get tired of talking about the weather, they rub their eyes and cough, their coughing a kind of comment.

The bar ditches are cracked with thirst, the wheat pinched. In town, the mayor announces that water will have to be rationed; unless it rains in the next few days, the lawns are doomed. The wind is blistering. Cicadas drop out of the trees, shrilling. The heat, the dryness, the cicadas, are a terrible itch. The cicadas are everywhere, they screech underfoot, falling like the rain that should, but does not, fall.

Early one morning, well before first light, Father Gilvary is awakened by the jangling of the phone. It takes him a full minute to decide that it isn't the alarm ringing, and another minute or two to set his feet moving in the right direction, the summons never letting up. He fumbles the receiver: "Hello, Saint Jude," scowling into it.

On the other end is a man who's thinking of killing himself. He might or he might not, he probably will. He'll surely do it if Father Gilvary calls the police. He speaks with the utmost calm, almost a pedantry. No, he'd rather not give his name, but he is willing to tell where he's at—corner of Line and Singletree, where the fairground starts. "Come and see," he says. Father Gilvary promises he'll be there directly. "Don't decide anything till I come. Give me fifteen minutes, hear? Hello? You still there? Good, yes, stay where you are. I'm on my way."

"Fifteen minutes . . ." The voice considers this. "Stay where you are."

Maybe a trick? Somebody's sick idea of a joke? Father Gilvary allows himself an instant of doubt.

Get cracking!

Father Gilvary has the streets to himself; it takes him less than ten minutes to make it to the gates. His eye roams the perimeter of the fairground: no one. He positions himself at the entrance and remains posted for several minutes. Nothing doing here. Then he moves past the empty ticket booth and enters the grounds.

Nothing here. The giant wheel of the Hurricane is stalled. Only eight arms, Father Gilvary notices, but they look like a hundred when the machine gets going. The empty passenger tubs sway on their fragile pins as the breeze takes them. The penny pitch and the shooting galleries are empty. There isn't a telephone booth in sight. And only one living person: a young boy stretched out on three folding chairs, next to a rack of air rifles and a giant bull's-eye. Sound asleep.

Lemonade stand for Line Street Baptist Church up ahead. He can make out the legend, from John 7:37, in foot-high letters: IF ANY MAN THIRST LET HIM COME TO ME AND DRINK. Crushed paper cups and corndog sticks litter the ground.

Do something! But what? In the trailers behind the booths, the shades are drawn. Only the breeze moves, scribbling the dust.

Start over.

Outside the fairground again, Father Gilvary repeats his circuit of the bordering streets. Then quits, heads for home. Maybe the man will call back, maybe he's been calling all this while, he could have changed his mind in the meantime. Father Gilvary settles in at his desk, waiting, his fingers splayed out, tensely stretched, the phone inches from his fingers. *In your mercy*–he tries to pray.

> *In your mercy and loving kindness*
> *no thought of ours is left unguarded,*
> *no tear unheeded, no joy unnoticed—*

But why should He pay attention? The supplications, the prayers are incessant. Sometimes Father Gilvary imagines the scene as a thicket of small brushfires, anxious smoke streaming upward from so many squatter's lots, a suffocating fog of desire rising, the din of petition, an infernal crackling . . .

He corrects himself, *Lord, I believe. Help my unbelief.*

Fifteen, twenty minutes, an hour passes. Do something! But what? Tell me what. He's damned if he does, damned if he doesn't.

He dials slowly, his face close to the numbers. The police officer at the recording end is calm, careful, unrushed. He asks twice: could Father Gilvary not recognize the voice? No? Not even a guess? He notes the time of the man's call, and makes no judgment on Father Gilvary's decision not to contact the police immediately. Some country western tune with weeping violins is playing in the background, something bittersweet about losing and feeling free. A string of losses–a saddle in Houston, a horse? a leg? a wife? in San Antone. The officer will be in touch if anything turns up. "Likewise, here," Father Gilvary promises, not in the least hopeful.

Wedged between the radio and the phone, Father Gilvary keeps vigil at his desk throughout the morning. He listens to the local news. The big story is weather: "Dryland farmers who are still waiting for moisture may be discouraged by the five-day forecast, but the weather should speed the curing of any fresh alfalfa crop . . ." He waits, through a five-minute discourse on Russian aphids, greenbugs and thrips.

Aside from the weather, there is the fair. Entries have dwindled, he learns, at the Open Rabbit Show. After the rabbits, come the lambs. The lambs, he is told, are lethargic. He listens with growing impatience to the roll call of winners and runners-up in the junior lamb category, the medium wool lamb, the fine wool lamb, to the long list of grand champion waterfowl honors.

How much longer?

He sits on through the culinary honor list for breads, for cakes not iced or glazed, for iced and decorated cakes, for cookies, jellies, pickles and relishes. Will it never end?

Livestock prices. He'll give it one more minute.

The minute's up and it's back to weather again. And that's quite enough—he's already on his feet—time to clear out. He'll catch up on his round of shut-ins. Day like today, it will be a relief.

Visiting Kathleen Macy—her joints all knotted up with arthritis—Father Gilvary worries about faithless prayer. By now she's exhausted the remedies and rumors of remedy. Last month it was cod liver oil: "Nasty, but it helps lubricate the joints through the blood system." . . . "I've heard bee stings help the pain," a few weeks before that. "If I really believed it, I'd stick my hand in the hive."

What they have left is prayer. Every visit, Father Gilvary prays for healing, for the chill, dead lumps in her joints to melt away, all the while knowing that it will not happen. Knowing, too, that if only he had faith the size of a grain of mustard seed–

Today she shows him a new swelling on her wrist, under the base of her thumb. "See, Father," she says, taking his hand, "how soft it is." The lump is spongy; it will become harder. Then Father Gilvary folds Kathleen's hands in his, closes his eyes and, as though he's moving in a dream, asking for her blessing, gently straightens and presses her fingers to his own eyelids. What does he feel? A counterpressure? A radiation? A warmth? He can feel life returning, a pulse–hers or his own, he cannot tell–then cords tightening, her fingers rigid, straining to free them-selves–*let go!* Her hands fall, clumps.

The shock of it! Father Gilvary murmurs, "I don't know what I was thinking of." Whatever next? He was thinking of nothing at all.

"Not feeling well?" Kathleen puts the best light on things. "You're not looking yourself these days, Father."

Not yourself . . . Same words Sue Penders used.

Back at the rectory, he buries the afternoon paper under an old *Sunday Visitor*. He busies himself at his desk, glancing up at the telephone at intervals. There are no calls.

It is so dry. Evenings, sitting at his open window, Father Gilvary listens to the din of the fair. He can make out a coppery glow in the distance, the rattle of tubs and the screams from the Hurricane–thin cries, scraped from

metal, meaningless, revolving through meaning—surprise, delight, distress, surprise . . .

He, too, is parched. Beyond sadness, really. Beyond feeling, almost; it's like nothing that's come before. As a young priest, and even past the time of his silver jubilee, he'd had attacks of what he called "the iffies," the "suppose that's," the "would have if's," flocks of regret at the little lights of possibility, one after another, going out. Lorena Miller, married these many years. Grandmother, probably, by now. Ruth Murchin gone off, who knew where. And Sister Rosalie?

Rosalie . . . How impossibly young they'd both been! And what was left of those few precious moments of aberration in the mimeographing closet, the clumsy kiss, the swift remorse, the tears in the confessional? A strengthening of resolve, they thought; together, they'd agreed never to allow "small dreams" to distract them from the great commitment.

Ruth Murchin had been something else altogether—a provocation without a temptation. He'd not handled that well. She'd wanted to become a nun, and, failing that, his mistress; that was how she'd propositioned him. She brought out all the cynicism in him, gave credence to the sour tales he'd heard down the years. How you could hang a clerical collar on anything, a fence post, and the women would come flocking to it. The attraction? They liked the prohibition, and the challenge: "no" means yes, wait and see!

It was Lorena who had shaken him; he realized what was happening to him in March. One of those days before spring when the tight shaking of the trees could be seen, a visible pulse along the shanks of the outermost branches, and in the knobs, the locked parcels of the leaves. Not trembling, but hard–a pounding. The tossing of the wind seemed idle and languid beside it. How strange, that he can no longer remember anything important from that time, only the sight of those trees, then a swarm of scruples–spending too much time with her alone, being seen together too often in public, distractions during prayer, a fever of yearnings (lumped under the rubric of "bad thoughts" for the purposes of Confession, and never detailed). What else? Only that his anguish was real–a shaking, a terrible loosening. What else? She was bookish, that he recalled. Had an odd, intent way of walking, as though she were looking for money on the ground. But– were her eyes hazel or green? He cannot remember. It was she who took action. Married, moved out of town, and settled things for him.

That had happened more than thirty years ago.

How he'd chafed at the myriad tiny cassock buttons that stood between the frailty of his flesh and the seductions of the world! He'd been told that he would. He'd been cautioned never to rest in his vigilance: not until ten minutes after death–it was a physiological fact–would he be truly safe at last.

And yet, not all the tempters were fearful–such was their subtlety. They had human faces, kind hearts, soft hands, disarming smiles. And minds. He'd been warned about this, too. But by now the iffy questions are moot, the temptations faded. His solitude is immaculate, his chastity perfect and perpetual. *Vacare Deo*–that was the point of celibacy–being free for God. Free? Or vacant? A vacancy for God. He has outlasted all the crises, the loneliness, the longing to drink, and the opposite longing –to pour himself out body and soul, a libation, to another body and soul.

These trials are over.

The weekend passes, the fair closes. Father Gilvary rakes the daily paper with a magnifying glass, page after page, column by column. On Tuesday, the *Durance Standard* prints an obituary for a man who isn't dead. On Thursday, that same man takes out an ad, a brief message in banner headlines:

JOHN PURCELL

I'M STILL ALIVE

All week–not a word about suicide, only the daily deaths by natural causes.

There's a change, though, in the air. Hard to put your finger on what it is, but it feels like something coming. Tonight; or tomorrow, early. People call it "falling weather." Something–whether mist, rain, or hail, no one can say–is going to fall. People keep glancing up at the sky, checking. Half an hour of hail would finish off the wheat for sure. The air is heavy, but not still. Too heavy for a breeze to ruffle it, yet unquiet. Freighted.

He runs his fingers along the spines of his books. He knows these by touch . . . the frayed Chesterton, Saint John Chrysostom, the Golden-mouthed, stiffly brocaded . . . Tanquerey's *Compendium Theologiae Dogmaticae* and the *History of the Councils,* so rarely opened, furred with a fine coating of dust . . . the Little Flower, scarcely a ripple, between the bulging concordances and commentaries.

Seeds and Seasons, The Hogan Schism, The Very Rich Hours . . . he'll miss them. He plucks one out–*Homily Hints for Ordinary Time*–and sits down with it. Spreads the fingers of his right hand, fanwise, across the cover. He still has a few options. "You might take a sightseeing trip," Dr. Stas suggested at the end of his last visit. "While you still can. Europe–or a tour of the Holy Land, why not?"

Why not? He has never seen the Holy Land.

He won't. No reason. Only a feeling, but strong to the point of certainty. This is where he is meant to be: Saint Jude's Church, Durance, Texas, in a dry season. Here he will learn . . . what? Whatever it is he is meant to learn.

It's not the way he'd dreamed it . . . All through seminary, his ambition had been for missionary work in darkest Africa or India–some lost, miasmal place, where his faith would be tested and, he hoped, strengthened. Then, after years of good works in the field–he wasn't rushing things–martyrdom, if he were worthy. *Bread for the teeth of lions.* To be ground down. How it would be, he'd never visualized precisely–whether by bullet, knife, car bomb or what. Let it be swift when it came was all he asked. No time to think, please God.

What egotism! And how exquisitely just the deflation . . . Swiftly, his single year of mission work in India had disabused him of all illusion. He'd spent most of the year in bed, confined to the infirmary. Dysentery, of all things. Shipped back to Chicago, he'd been counseled on knowing his limitations and working within them.

He'd been crushed at the time, but learned to joke about it later: "I was ready for martyrdom. It was the rice, day in and day out, I couldn't bear." He still sought a place where he wouldn't be too comfortable. Hardship conditions–he hadn't backed down on that–but in the States, somewhere beyond the snug Catholic enclaves of the big cities.

Which brought him out to Molina, Texas, on the High Plains. Foreign enough to make him homesick for Chicago–it surprised him how desolate he felt. For the first time he was on his own. Priests in the Diocese of Letsem City lived many miles apart. Most had mission churches in addition to their regular parishes; they gathered together only for Clergy Day during the summer and the annual Chrism Mass during Holy Week.

Then came Killern, Randall, and now Durance, his fourth and final assignment–what meaning is he to find in coming to such a place? And, having come and seen for himself, of persisting here?

It had been an accidental town from the very start. "Named for what?" he'd asked when he arrived, thinking it must be "endurance," endurance against the odds, for what other distinction could it claim to have? He'd been close, as it turned out, but not exact. In fact the town had been named not for a "what" but a "who"–in honor of its first settler, Jack Durance, a cattle driver on his way to Kansas, who'd been forced to a halt here when the weather became impassable. He'd built a dugout and hunkered down for the duration. Returned to the same spot to ranch a few years after that. Over the decades, he'd been followed by people passing through on their way elsewhere, whose water, or money, or gas, ran out.

Accidental . . . yet holding. Buried in the Dust Bowl, resurrected in the oil boom, now, fallen again on hard times, the Chamber of Commerce dreaming of hi-tech industry but willing to welcome what the newspaper called "a little manufacture of whatever kind." Waiting for Jesus to stake his claim on the territory, expecting Him any moment, but, in the meantime, scratching on somehow. Occupying till He came. Durable, unkillable—a hard place.

Sometimes, Father Gilvary felt as though he were living on the outermost rim of the earth. The flat emptiness of the land appalled him at first, the omnipresence, the vast expectancy, of the sky. A stage waiting for actors, props, to appear, the key scene to unfold. Against this backdrop, all the legions of the saints might appear, jostling rank upon rank, like a breaking in of waters, and no one be surprised. Although he saw nothing but an immense scaffolding, sun, cloud drift, dust, Father Gilvary understood how it was when, from time to time, one of his parishioners, gazing skyward, saw Jesus, mantled in light, standing on a pillar of air, or afloat, arms out, surfing the clouds, birds dipping beneath his feet. Kildees, they would be, but in the guise of doves, plumped by the hungering eye.

By now, Father Gilvary wouldn't choose, and—to be honest—would be unfit to live in any other place. The last time he visited Chicago, for Katie's funeral, was six or seven years ago. Or even eight? Whatever . . . a good many years back. He felt caged in the city, crimped to a merely human scale. He hated the noise, the press, the grime, the buildings tall in their own conceit. And he felt himself an outsider, a stranger among nieces and nephews he'd never known. Katie was the last, the last of his batch, brothers and sisters all gone now; he had no reason, no desire really, to ever go back to Chicago again.

So here he is, for the duration.

It's too hard to read, too early for bed. Trying to pray, Father Gilvary's mind wanders. What now? Television? He is reduced to that. He runs through the channels, settles on the news.

An ordinary day in ordinary time. A litter of corpses and gutted cars fills the screen. Somewhere in the rubble of Beirut, alongside the ruins of a hospital, an old man in Arab headdress has set up a stand selling sandbags, transistor radios, and Coca-Cola. He shrugs into the camera, says something they do not bother to translate, and the scene shifts. So much for that–that's how many?–four? five?– seconds on Lebanon. On with the next. A blizzard of green: foliage and gunfire in some Latin American nation. Father Gilvary blinked and now he's lost the name of it. Lost the thread. Children with automatic rifles prowl the streets of a village. *The reign of God is already in your midst.* Somehow. The anchorman and his assistant are now passing the time of day with one another.

Now what? Must be electrical interference. The picture shrinks to a stripe. The stripe shimmies upward and disappears. Reappears at the bottom of the screen and travels up. Disappears. Reappears. Crackles. Father Gilvary walks over and slaps the side of the console several times, with vigor. The picture slows, steadies, expands. It's Pete Whatsis, the anchorman, jabbing a colored map.

Plans for the celebration of a cosmic Harmonic Convergence are underway, he announces. Whatever that might be. It must have been explained during Father Gilvary's electrical difficulties. On—when?—he missed the date. Sometime coming up. People will be standing on hills all over the world, holding hands and humming. Albuquerque will be one of the vibrational centers. Something to do with the convergence of Venus and Pluto, the dawn of a new age, a fresh seeding of the universe.

While back on earth, the harvest continues: a decapitation in Childress, the head and nude body of the female victim found miles apart; a school for skydivers in Letsem City—the graduates drop out of the air, hung by their hats, looks like, waving; an infant found at the Safeway on Line Street; two lost in a grain elevator fire on Farm-to-Market Road; an ad for fried chicken batter. What does it all mean? Anything? Who composed these things? Who got them together? Or were they thrown together?

Enough. It's not worth waiting for weather.

Early to bed, he decides, and has already begun to undress when he hears, he's almost sure, someone at the door. A light, but persistent, tapping; it isn't the wind. He shuffles down the hall in stocking feet, working the buttons of his shirt as he goes. Of course he gets the sequence wrong—he's skipped one—or more? No time to check. Bluff it.

It's Sue Penders with a pie plate full of brownies, fresh from the oven. To the ends of the earth she would pursue him, bearing her pie plate.

"Won't you come in?" She won't, he trusts. His fingers creep to his open collar: hopelessly awry.

"No, no. Not to trouble you," she says.

"Mm . . . Isn't this a nice surprise!" He lifts the plate—a thick sludge of sweetness fills his nostrils. "Fresh baked!" She means well, but what's on her mind?

"Now you eat that while it's fresh, Father. I don't want to find it sitting around in your icebox a month from now. It's made from scratch, all the best ingredients. Think you've been losing a little weight lately—"

"Not so," says Father Gilvary, smiling and thumping his waist. "Brisket to the core."

"Now, Father! Everything all right with you? Really?"

"Everything but this heat we've been having lately. Seems to be letting up a little, though. I can't recall another drouth quite like this." Stave her off, she's fishing.

"Father?"

The breeze has begun to kick up.

"You do look tired, you know. You don't mind my saying so? I'm not the only one that's noticed, but I'm the only one that'll tell it to your face. You ought to take a break. We all need vacations from time to time. Even you."

Father Gilvary smiles. "And I will. I most certainly will. I'm planning on it. Sometime in the fall. Isn't this breeze nice!"

"Lovely, yes. I won't let you forget now. Night, Father."

"Night."

She'd been fishing, all right. Didn't miss a thing: the

mismatched buttons, his standing there in his socks; he can just hear her at the Legion of Mary. "Hasn't been looking himself for a long time," she'd begin. "Not since Lee Waring died." A legion of pie plates would follow.

Plate in hand, Father Gilvary lingers at the open door. The air is definitely cooler now, and the moon, a sliver, is flat on its back, like a saucer waiting for a cup. You don't often catch that angle of moon. "Wet moon," they call it, ready to hold rain.

He sleeps brokenly. Dreams and wakes, and cannot remember what he dreams. Except for one—it's so clear.

He's on a freight elevator—a featureless space, enclosed in walls of unpainted steel. The elevator is full of passengers to start. Strangers all. Rising, something falls in the pit of his stomach; descending, it soars; coming to a halt, it floats . . . an eerie, weightless feeling. It occurs to Father Gilvary that no one has ever pushed a button, there is nothing to push, no control panel. They rise, descend, rise again. The door opens and a passenger gets off. No one speaks. Another passenger gets on. Father Gilvary turns and asks the woman next to him where she's getting off. She tells him that she'll know when she gets there. She gets off. Down they go. The door opens and Father Gilvary gets off. His feet are supported though he cannot see how. The dark is bottomless. There are no boundaries, no ceiling or walls. No landmarks at all. He's shouting, "There's nothing out here!"—when a voice booms back at him. "I'm talking to you, Tommy, you hear me?" His father's voice. "You were right, Dad, there's nothing out here," he calls back. The voice comes again:

"How can you say there's nothing out here when I'm talking to you, Tommy?"

Something moving outside. The curtains are blowing out into the yard, flags, a signal that he's left the window wide open. Not very wise. Father Gilvary steps lightly across the room, leans against the sill, and listens.

Cattle truck, speeding down the Interstate. He can tell it is empty by its windy clatter, but it is not this sound that holds his attention, it is something closer–a shuddering of air, the sound of damp breathing–

Horses cropping grass. On the rectory lawn!

Impossible–he must still be dreaming.

But it is so clear. There, where the shadows are clumped, he can see them nuzzling the earth, drinking from the low, scattered fountains of the grass, can hear the shifting of their hooves, the plicking of strings, of many threads breaking. It is perfectly clear.

The rain is starting to come down.

Rain

Val wakes to the noise of somebody working the roof over with sticks. He makes his way to the window nearest him and looks out. There is nothing to see: the rain beats down, blackening walls already dark. Some drops hit the sill, his hands on the sill— a few sharp splats. He stiffens, slams down one window, then the other.

All tight.

Now, where was he? He cannot step back into whatever it was he was dreaming. Something about sleeping under a car and waking up. He dreamed he'd woken up: he couldn't see a thing, it was dark, the ceiling low.

And now the voices come to him.

Your answer is you don't remember?

He's trying to remember. Asks himself: how many closets did the apartment– That should get things rolling. He's going to walk through the foyer in his mind, and keep on walking, past the dining area, on into the bedroom . . .

Walk. Don't run.

Says to himself: my shirt is on the chair by the bed. He sees it: the ladderback chair, his shirt thrown over the top rung. Wallet is in the third drawer of the dresser, left-hand side, under the socks–it's perfectly clear.

Open the wallet. Now take a look inside. There they are: cards, photos, everything in place. The money untouched. What was he looking for?

He's forgotten.

What he remembers best is the view from his bedroom window in New York: a drugstore, an iron grating over the window by night. The Rx sign has a mortar and pestle under it, made of neon lights. The pestle is meant to move, but something is screwed up in the signals so the flow of light is broken. The three mixing positions have become three separate pestles, stalled–one standing, one leaning, one nearly tipped over. Why does a detail like this hang on, while everything that really counts evaporates? Something so useless–

Your memory was better then, wasn't it?

I don't remember.

Sometimes the voices in his head get so loud he can't hear the voice next to his ear, can't see the face in front of him. "You hear what I'm saying?" Henrietta will blast at him. He hears her, he's not deaf.

I loved what I bought–I remember that.

And that's all he remembers. It's like a power outage. He sees the wallet, expensive burgundy leather, nesting in a drawer full of balled-up socks and folded handkerchiefs. A moment back, he opened the wallet in his mind . . .

Just thinking about it tires him out, makes him want to sleep for a long time.

The rain is quieter, he notices, soft and steady, yet relentless, it moves like fingers smoothing creases, running along the seams of his mind.

I really care.

How does she say it now in what voice? Who to?

It's over before dawn. So quiet now, Val can hear the clock yakking to itself, the chairs listening. He turns on the radio and waits for the weather report. "Friendly skies are coming back," the weatherman says.

Most days at the restaurant, they're just waiting around. Waiting for rain to fall, for the price of wheat or oil to soar, waiting for rescue, for Jesus to drop out of the clouds, waiting for love to come into their dreary lives, waiting for night, for morning, for death.

But this morning, for a change, something has arrived. And they're savoring. Place is full of crazies and queers, as usual, and the rain has loosened them up even more than usual. Here's one of the regulars who hasn't said a thing before in Val's hearing beyond what he wants off the menu–suddenly, he's got words to spare. "Got to shake the dew off my lily," he says, winking, getting up to take a leak.

And there's that one over there in the far corner, old Black Suit, whispering to himself, slicing the air over his cinnamon twist. Same thing same time every morning. When he looks over Val's way, it's catty corner, squinting. Then he smiles into his cup like he's on to something. What? What exactly?

"Today is my anniversary," one of the ancients pipes up, the only one who seems glum this truly fine morning. Nobody listening, so she says it again, louder. "My husband passed on exactly one year ago today. Lost my husband to Death. A year ago this day."

Now what are you supposed to say to that?

It's an embarrassment, even here, and only Henrietta would be dumb enough to try and answer it. "I wish you well, Mary," she says.

Their jokes are the saddest he's ever heard. Senseless. There's one about a Vietnamese rancher. "A Vietnamese rancher's got what? Two dogs? That's a ranch for them." That gets snorts of laughter all around. When Val doesn't join in, the joker gets a little nervous. "Some Vietnamese live on my block," he adds. "Hard working–I don't hold anything against them. We don't mix with them much, is all. I mean, they sort of live for each other a lot, you know. And they're sort of strange to us, other people, I mean."

Mix–don't mix, Val could care less. It's a nothing town. Place to lick your wounds, stash some money (nothing to spend it on), and split.

He's tired of hearing about the old times, what a hard place this was. How they ate bare mustard on bread when they were hungry as kids. He's heard it all–how they had to put out prairie fires by spilling the blood of their herds, having no water to spare. How they fought the wind, the blowing dust.

"Started out as a speck in the mud," the old-timers keep saying, like it's gone on to great heights since. They love to dwell on those small beginnings. "Kind of town where everytime the streetlight changed a bell would ring. Now that's the mark of a hick town. There wasn't a whole lot going on, back then. It was all prairie. Grass and a little wind."

Greatest thing that ever happened was way back in 1903. Jack Price, who was mayor then, had a vision and hired a surveyor with a mule-drawn plow to plow a single furrow from Raton to Durance to show folks how to get into town.

The second greatest thing was a shoot-out between a white cowboy and a black that very same year. And the special thing about that was: they both had the same name: Sam Bates. These facts don't mean chickenshit to Val—they are nothing he ever wanted to know—but they are what he remembers. It's crazy, when what matters most to him is gone clean beyond recall. Vanished.

In one way, Val knows he has it good here. The work is light compared to meat packing, and when quitting time comes he's quit of it. The tips aren't lavish, but the food is decent; he eats well. He's stocking up, and not just on hash and hamburger. Stella saves some of the prime cuts for him. The beef here is special—fresh kill, you can taste the difference.

Back at the house, it's close. He left the windows shut this morning. Forgot about that. The air in the hallway, in his room, is stale. Hard to name what it is . . . something burnt, rice maybe, some trace of burning, a memory fading, from yesterday or the day before.

Val stands at the window: there's a blister in the glass. At first he thinks it's water and tries to wipe it off, but, no, it's hard, clear, and fixed. If he opens the window, he knows what he'll get. But he needs air.

Sure enough, he can hear the creaking of bone and wood. All the old biddies are sitting out on the porch, drinking up the cool, rocking and clacking in the breeze. Men on the one side–there are but two, women on the other. It's the men talking now. Rain is still the big event.

"Got up at five. About when the rain left off. I was coughing. Said to myself, 'Why waste gas?' So then I went back to bed till six."

"Six-thirty's my speed, rest my old bones."

"Why say 'old bones'?"

"What are they if they aren't old bones?"

And on and on and on . . .

First he sees threads, then ghostly ropes, then sheets flung down. Rain at last.

In the morning there are new streams everywhere. Cleat cannot believe that the heat was only yesterday, cannot rightly remember the dry dusty weeks that came before.

At the post office, he learns that Betty and Buck are going to Muleshoe for the weekend. They're taking the Chevy pickup and leaving the Dodge. Cleat has keys to the house and knows that the extra car keys are kept in the white china kettle with the broken spout. He has an idea.

It's a few minutes before five when Cleat drives up to the restaurant. He parks and sits with his motor idling for a little bit, then ventures inside. Walks up to the counter, but doesn't sit down.

When Val comes by, he says, "How about a ride?"

"On what, a camel?" asks Val. "You got wheels suddenly?"

"Thought you might be dying to get out."

"Well, I might," says Val. And he lets it be known that he's off at seven. "You might swing by then."

"I'll drive," says Val. Cleat scoots over to the passenger side. Fine by him.

It's a four-door, and Cleat has opened all the windows to catch the breeze. Out in the open country, you can feel the coolness coming up out of the ground. A real gully washer, that was, the downpour last night. The bar ditches are full, the fields spotted with playa lakes, clean blue, like patches of sky. When the prairie begins to roll, it looks like the sea, rising, swelling and falling back. The breeze is cool, there's something green in the air, the air tastes and smells green.

Kildees skimming. "Hear them?"

Val doesn't say a thing. He's holding the wheel with one hand, Cleat notices; his other hand's gone from trailing out the window to resting on the ledge. Cleat gazes at the dark hairs on Val's wrist, reddish in the light. Then he tries to look off at a windmill spinning in the distance. He wonders if the silence is going on too long.

"That's rare," Cleat observes, "somebody planting fence to fence. Most people leave out one third of the land. It restores the soil." He sounds like a tour guide, even in his own ears.

Cleat wants to ask Val: when it's raining do you have the feeling it's raining all over the world, like I do? And when the sun is shining do you have the feeling it's shining all over the world? Instead, he blurts out another question, the one he's been saving to ask at a later time:

"What do you think of me?"

"Nothing," says Val. "What should I think?"

"Do you like working in the restaurant?"

"It sucks," says Val.

"Why do you stay then?"

"Why do you ask dumb questions?"

The land levels out. Cattle coming up, white-faced Herefords, maybe a thousand head. They look half-human. There's a brew of manure, mud, steaming fur and rotting silage in the air. Feedlot. Val's racing past. He isn't even looking ahead, Cleat realizes, but into the rearview mirror —he's driving by what's behind him!—racing to get that feedlot out of his sight.

They're whipping along, it's like dreaming, like boarding an express train, watching the doors slide shut. There's no way out. Cleat doesn't want out, even though he knows that soon, not far down the road, they're going to crash.

Let it be together is all Cleat asks. He stares at the tunnel of Val's ear, then at Val's face, the half of it, all he can see. Val looks like he's fixing to plow a section, squinting away off down the field to plan how the furrows go. The needle of the speedometer swoops forward pointing at Cleat, then down past him. At eighty, it shivers, it's starting to break. Gas pedal must be down to the floor now. Cleat bites his lip: not one word. Air hisses rushing by–if he trails his arm over the window ledge like he usually does, he'll be sucked out. He needs to think but there isn't time, fence posts flick past, blend, topple in heaps behind them. They're fishtailing, the lane divider is swinging. Two lanes, no traffic, but they're veering, they're gobbling the yellow line–

Cleat clamps his eyes shut.

They're leaving the earth behind.

"I feel sick," the words leak from his lips.

"Not in here." Val hits the brakes.

Cleat's hurled to the dash. Then back. Against Val. It's fast, bright, blinding– The steering wheel slams into his face.

When the light breaks he sees: fence post and pump, and furred, a tagged brown ear . . . Dust boiling up.

"Cleat?"

Another face leaning in soft slippery as a cloud and fixed in that face are–teeth!–the bright square stones, a dark open wound–a mouth–

"Hey, Cleat?" The light is winking.

His glasses are twisted, pressed into his nose. There's sand in his throat and in his ears a grindy gravelly ringing slows and deepens. Knocks. This thought comes to him: press: knock: I am knocking.

He wants to be rooted, to curl in. To be housed. When he slammed against the wheel, he felt the tight bones at Val's shoulder and chest, his heart lurched. He touched Val.

"You okay, Cleat?"

It was worth everything.

A Mighty Wind

Three ticks to go till the hour. She'll never hear it.

It's middle of a Thursday morning and Stella is humming along with the radio, it's Willie Nelson singing "Hello Walls," and Honeybun Chesem is saying how daylight savings time isn't God's time or natural time but a meddling with both, and Henrietta feels time of any kind hanging heavy on her hands. There's nobody around but the help, and Honeybun, who's getting mouthier by the minute, when in comes Brother Shad and Brother Burch, the youth minister. They're both togged out in their Sunday best, three-piece suits, dark blue. White shirts, cuffs, maroon ties.

Henrietta lets them know it's a red-letter occasion having them, but they're not staying, they want two coffees to go. "Lord's business," is all Brother Shad will say about it, and he drums his fingers on the register table so hard that the little shot glass with the toothpicks goes ajitter.

"Sad about Sister Willodene," says Henrietta. "Just when she was looking so robusk."

Brother Shad nods, shuts his eyes and slants his head, like he's listening to a little small voice that's coming from his collarbone. Henrietta figures he's praying, so quits jabbering. Or maybe it's her makeup—bending his eyes away from that. She knows Brother Shad does not approve of vanities. Fact is, he's never seen her done up full strength before. On Wednesday nights, she comes faded after a long day's work, and on Sundays she just dabs it—just enough so she can stand herself. So maybe that's why his head's tucked down now, chastising her. But maybe not. Maybe Brother Shad's got other things on his mind. And, really, there's no harm in fixing her face: it peps her up, and gives people something cheerful to look at. It's a courtesy, is what it is. That's how she views it. She picks up a pile of receipts and pretends she's checking them over. Brother Shad's still standing there, as he was; he might be sleeping on his feet.

He comes quickly back to life, though, once Val returns with his order. Henrietta checks the lids on the Styrofoam cups and lowers them into a sack. "I've been meaning to visit with Sister Willodene, God rest her soul," she says. She adds sugar, creamer, stirrers and nap-

kins. "I plan to be out at the burying, of course," she promises them.

"Wait and see," Brother Burch smiles. "Never a problem too big for Jesus," he says. "Never a problem too small. The word of God is a living, breathing instrument." That's when Henrietta gets the idea that they're fixing to make a miracle.

Father & Son is right around the corner from Henrietta's restaurant. Not worth reparking, really, so Brother Shad and Brother Burch haul out a few things from the car and make their way over on foot. Brother Shad carries their best Bibles, the ones with the white leatherette covers and glittery gold edges. Brother Burch brings the coffee, a blanket and a ladies' overnight case.

The building is two-storied with a wraparound porch. No signs of activity anywhere on the premises. The shades on the second floor are drawn.

Mounting the porch steps, Brother Shad declares, "The voice of the Lord is amplified in me. In the last days, He shall pour out His spirit upon all flesh."

"Glory!" Brother Burch affirms it.

"The Lord wants to use us in a mighty way." Brother Shad whispers, pacing with impatience, as they wait in the lobby. They've set their things down on the low table that holds stacks of paper tissues, smelling salts, prayer cards, and pre-need burial application forms. Father & Son has been in the business since Durance was founded, same family handed down, and serving everybody in town, all the denominations, even the Hard Shells, the Full Flame, and the Holiness crowd. Even the Romans. Whatever qualms Brother Shad might have about this array, he trusts the Lord to know his own.

But here's Fred Sharp, in rumpled gardening clothes. "Morning, Reverends," he greets them, "a little early, aren't you?"

Brother Shad explains how they want to pray over Sister Willodene.

"Why, yes, help yourselves," Fred invites them. "She's all ready and waiting, pretty as a picture. But, gentlemen, you know it's well before noon. The viewing's not till three-thirty."

"We'd like to have a quiet spell to pray over her," Brother Shad says. "She was such a Spirit-filled Christian lady."

After shutting the door of the viewing room, Brother Shad draws the bolt softly. He makes a slow circuit of the premises. There are three windows: one of stained glass, rose and gold, that does not move; two of clear glass that stand open to the garden. Brother Shad goes over to the clear windows, shutting and latching them. He draws the heavy white drapes, making sure they overlap in the middle. The casket is supported by a draped metal stand. Flanking it on either side are three folding chairs. These, Brother Shad shoves back to the walls, saying, "Got to give the lady room." There's a vase of yellow roses on a tripod posed at the head of casket, an elaborate plastic wreath at the foot.

"I've got me a conviction," Brother Shad sings out. "He's gonna split the clouds–"

"I can't hardly wait," Brother Burch seconds it. "I'm in a state of ex-treme anticipation."

Sister Willodene, stretched out on white satin, does not yet share their excitement. She rides high in her bed, her hands cupped over foam rubber supports, her lips stretched in the thinnest of smiles. "And I dare you," her lips seem to say.

But nothing is impossible with the Lord. Brother Shad removes his jacket and his vest, drapes them carefully on the back of one of the chairs, then loosens his tie. Brother Burch does the same, releasing his collar button as well, and rolling up his sleeves. Brother Shad is the first to kneel at the side of the casket. "Roll away the stone, Lord," he pleads. "For us, it is too heavy to lift, but with your help, we can do all things."

"Brother Burch, do you see the color rising to her cheeks?"

"Glo-ry!" from Brother Burch. For the color does seem to be rising. Rising to the cheeks of Brother Shad as well, and to the white satin that lines the casket, and to the rose and gold window overhead.

"Brother Burch, will you anoint her, please?"

Brother Burch takes a dab of the lotion on his forefinger and applies himself to Sister Willodene's brow and hands. He intones:

"Oh, glory to your name, Jesus!

Glo-ry to your name.

Glory to your name, Jesus!"

"Oh, my my my my!" declares Brother Shad. "We're gonna pray outselves up a storm. Let's have a little more oomph, Brother Burch. In Je-sus' mighty name!"

"All ri-ght!" Brother Burch throws himself into it: "Lord, we're gonna have us a prayer meeting, we're gonna pray harder than we ever prayed before. It's gonna be a red hot prayer, Lord, a prayer that comes from the tips of our toenails! It's gonna roll up out of us, we're gonna pray with all our hearts, our souls, our minds and our muscles. And, God Almighty, I know your Spirit's gonna come down in this place and give us an answer, an assurance, a divine assurance. You're gonna take care of this situation, Lord, completely and totally. We're calling on You, Lord, we're praying the effectual fervent prayer of James, chapter five. We know, Lord, there's a tremendous power resident in that kind of praying."

"There's no power on earth like the effectual fervent prayer of James, chapter five." Brother Shad is on his feet now, his arms upraised. "I feel—I feel a mighty wind aloose—"

"Oh, hear it!" says Brother Burch.

"Lord, with your power, I built your house. I stood on prairie. I saw the brick, the color, the roofline, before the foundation was laid. I saw the paneling on the wall . . ." Brother Shad is on his knees again. "I want to give You all the glory, all the honor. Glory to your name, Lord! Lord, raise up this Holy Ghost-filled Christian lady. Please, Lord. We have need of a miracle, Lord. Like that rain, after we'd been dry so long—"

"You can do it, Lord!" Brother Burch throws his head back, claps his hands.

But Sister Willodene isn't stirring yet.

"Let's just touch down a moment," suggests Brother Shad. "Time out. How 'bout a sip of coffee, Brother Burch?" The coffee is lukewarm by now, but it's energizing. They stand on either side of the casket, gazing down on Sister Willodene. Both are silent, glum.

A woman's glory is her hair—how often Brother Shad has preached it! Sister Willodene still has her rich crown of hair. You can tell that it once was gold, though now it is the color of dry straw. It is dressed in great detail as it was in life, swatches of hair lifted from the sides and nape of her neck and rolled, puffed, pinned and lacquered into place. In life, it managed to look like one head of hair, but today it seems piecemeal, patched.

Then Brother Shad sets down his cup decisively and leans over the casket. It is time to raise his voice: "Clap your hands, Sister Willodene, *make a joyful noise unto the Lord!* Don't be afraid to quake under the Spirit. You're demonstrating God's power to heal—to surprise—"

To be sure, the casket does seem to be shaking a little. Brother Shad is gripping the edge intently. And shouting now, "That's it, Willodene! A little clap in your hands, a little bounce to your feet! Lift up your voice. Oh, Willy! You can do it. The Lord wants you to rise."

At that very moment, they are interrupted by a tumultuous knocking.

A summons—

The door! Fred Sharp's voice on the other side of it: "Everything all right in there?"

Brother Burch assures him that everything's fine.

"Well, please pray a little softer," says Sharp, "my wife has a bad headache."

They wait until his footsteps die away.

Then Brother Shad leans close to Sister Willodene's ear, his voice nearly a whisper. "Please, Willy, open your eyes. Don't let your heart be troubled, good sister. The Lord has laid His hand upon you. He wants to bless you in a special way."

But Sister Willodene isn't batting an eyelash. Her lids are closed, save for a steely glimmer of white between the lashes.

"Got the specs, Brother Burch?"

Brother Burch pats his pockets without result.

"Oh, I know!"

Here they are, right where they should be—in the overnight case, wrapped up in her shawl. Brother Burch breathes damply on each lense, then wipes them clear with his handkerchief.

"Gently!" warns Brother Shad as Brother Burch hooks the eyeglasses around one ear, then the other, taking care not to muss the elaborately dressed hair.

"Look at me, Sister Willodene," commands Brother Shad. "Unseal in Jesus' name!"

Not a flutter. With spectacles on, Sister Willodene's eyes seem, if anything, doubly shut.

"Now, then, I want you to lay hands upon her, Brother Burch." Brother Shad takes Sister Willodene's left shoulder, Brother Burch her right. Brother Shad says firmly, "Sister Willodene, I know you are not dead but sleeping. Sister, arise!"

But around Sister Willodene the living press in vain. Although the casket rocks a little, like a frail boat, from the gusts of prayer besetting it on either side, Sister Willodene will not be roused.

And now Brother Shad lets go of Sister Willodene and slumps down. Pressing his cheek to the rim of the casket, he begins to weep hoarsely. "I've . . . walked . . . I've walked around this mountain long enough, Lord. Let me stand on the mountaintop for once, Lord. Let me stand on the mountaintop. Just once. It's been so long, Lord. Keep remembering how it was when You walked the earth, and the apostles after You—when the blind saw, the lame walked, the dead leaped up. I don't want to forget that You can raise and You can heal. Been a long time, Lord . . ."

Brother Burch's eyelids are tightly shut. He drums on the side of the casket and calls, *"Talitha*–come! Little sister, arise! Come forth, Sister Willodene–"

"Gentlemen! Gentlemen–open up!" A fist, then the flat of a hand pounds the door. "What's going on? Open up!" More hammering. The knob is pulled, twisted, the shaking of the door grows louder. "Do I have to call the police? I've got a profession to uphold. Are you deaf in there?"

Farther Along

INTENSIVE–Father Gilvary would know where he was with his eyes shut. As soon as he opens the door to the corridor, he hears the shirring of a respirator, two long senseless syllables said over and over, and the muffled pounding of a suction machine.

First he checks in at the nursing station. The patient is conscious. "Won't be long, though."

Room 33. Father Gilvary stands at the open door, on the threshold, clearing his throat by way of announcing his arrival. There is no answering sound. He leans into the room. He can make out the blackness of an open mouth, a gold tooth gleaming. The white face is tipped back; tubes and wires run into the sheets.

"John?" Father Gilvary makes his way quietly past the monitoring console. There is no bed table, so he unpacks his kit on the bed. Chrism, cotton wool, pyx—no time to lose. For the past week, John has eaten nothing but what Father Gilvary has given him: fragments of host.

"Father?"

"I'm right beside you, John."

"Grease me up good, Father."

"I will, I will!"

He seems restless as Father Gilvary anoints his hands, so Father Gilvary rings for the nurse. The injection takes hold at once. John turns to him then, "Save souls, Padre." It's his old send-off; this time, though, his voice is without body. Father Gilvary bends an ear to catch what he says next.

"It'll be all right. I'm ready for it, whatever it is. The next thing." His lips continue to shape air, but the rest is inaudible.

Peace is my farewell to you. Father Gilvary draws up a chair alongside and waits. *My peace is my gift to you.* He presses John's hand: it is dry and cool.

I do not give it as the world gives peace.

Seems to be sleeping now. Father Gilvary packs up his kit, folds his stole into it and moves on.

Father Gilvary glances up from his desk. There it goes again. A branch, maybe, played by the wind, scraping the casement? Or somebody at the door, dusting it with his fingertips, afraid to knock?

He makes his way to the door in time to find Cletus,

the postmaster's boy, backing off–already halfway down the steps. "I'm here," Father Gilvary calls to him, "but not as quick as I was. It takes me a while. Something I can do?"

"I thought–I just wanted to talk, that's all."

Father Gilvary waves the boy inside. "Why don't you sit here," he suggests, thumping the back of a padded chair. He drags forward his own chair, well free of the desk. "Thirsty?" he asks.

The boy doesn't answer. He sits, taut from head to toe. He sheds his cap. There's something on his forehead– badge, looks like, bruise, some discoloration. Or maybe the color's bled out from his cap? The boy takes off his glasses, folds them into his pocket, rubs his eyes. Father Gilvary has never seen the boy without his glasses, and cannot make out much now beyond the restless roaming of his eyes. Yet there is a sort of speaking in their feverish movement, Father Gilvary thinks. *My soul dwelling abroad in the eye of my flesh* . . . Be alert to it.

Half past. Silence, but for the scraping of the overhead fan, the ticking of the clock.

An odd creature, Father Gilvary has always felt, a land fish, something not quite– Best not to hurry him. He'll come round in his own good time. Or he won't come round. No use trying to force him.

Father Gilvary has always wondered about the boy's name. Who but a Catholic–a Catholic of the old school– would burden a child with such a name? Saint Cletus, or Anacletus, was Saint Peter's second successor in the Holy See, but how many people knew that?

Father Gilvary along with everyone else has been a recipient of the boy's handouts. Amazing, the number of people in town—and not only ministers—who seem to have a direct telephone line to God. The boy's "messages" are not original, they're a familiar mixture of slogan and scripture—news of Christ's speedy return, exhortations to repentance and readiness—standard fare for Durance. Some are catchier than others. Father Gilvary recalls one that asked: *If you were suspected of being a Christian and arrested for it, would there be enough evidence to convict you?* Nothing that hadn't been said, and better, before him.

A strange case . . . haunted and haunting. Used to hang around Saint Jude's years ago, until Father Gilvary wondered whether he might have a vocation. The postmaster was Baptist, though; he'd raised the boy Baptist, and he put a swift end to those visits.

"What I want to know is can you like somebody too much?" The business is out in a single breath.

"How do you mean 'like'?" Go slow, Father Gilvary cautions himself, feel your way.

"You know." The glasses are back now.

"I'm not sure I do. You mean 'love'?"

The boy twists the bright cloth of his cap between his fingers.

"Not if it is love," says Father Gilvary. But, no, he reflects as soon as he says it, that isn't so. You can love too much, he knows. He thinks about grieving, hating, loving, how alike they are—the searing, the same unnatural contraction of the world, the mind turning and turning on its pivot of pain.

But there was—he'd only glimpsed what it might be—another kind of love that burned without consuming, where that one peers out through my eyes, I through his. Years back, he'd tried to tell this to a boy hopelessly in love with a girl who'd deserted him. Father Gilvary had nearly been run out of town for the effort. It had been a terrible misunderstanding. "There are many kinds of love, and many counterfeits–a world of faking," is all Father Gilvary will permit himself to say to Cletus now. He's guessing, groping in the dark–

And now, suddenly, he feels that the conversation–monologue, really–has taken a wrong turn. Nothing he can point to, only a vague, yet growing, sense of uneasiness. A loose hunch–it must be wrong.

Can't be.

"It's unfair," Cletus says finally.

"It is unfair," Father Gilvary agrees. "Most love–what people call 'love'–is unequal. One always loves more."

Cletus is tensed forward, waiting to hear more. Keep it general. "We are all broken and in need of healing," Father Gilvary adds. This is a formula and perfectly safe.

No way of telling what the boy is thinking. Only his hands move, twisting, his eyes, shifting, never settling.

If it's that waiter Cletus has in mind, the one that calls himself "Val," then it's a sad, sad mistake. But it can't be, Father Gilvary tells himself.

Yet why not? It would be perfectly understandable, in a way: Val's a blank screen for anyone to dream on. But a mistake–there's nothing Val can give, even by way of casual friendship. He's a man on the run. Mornings in the restaurant, when Father Gilvary has looked Val's way, what he's seen is a blur of motion, the shadow of a man, his face half-erased; and he knows it's an accurate image, not a trick of his failing sight.

"I want to work," Cletus breaks in, "work till I'm so tired I can't think anymore."

"Come by Saturday," Father Gilvary offers. "I think I can find plenty of yard work for you."

And that seems to do it. The boy rises, mumbles thanks and steps out from the gray vestibule into the green light of evening.

John's wake, a simple rosary, is over. Tomorrow's Mass of the Resurrection will be more demanding.

Father Gilvary sits by his open bedroom window, legal pad on his lap, magic marker in hand, trying to decide on a text. A line from Romans—*Death has no more power over him*—comes to mind. And no wonder. How many times has he used it before? Think again.

He knows what he feels:

> *Like a weaver You have rolled up my life;*
> *You cut me off from the loom.*

It would never do, of course. "False start," he could see Father Glavin shaking his head. James Urban Glavin, of blessed memory . . . Otherwise known as plain "Jug," or "Urban." They'd split "a bourbon on Urban" at his wake. Father Glavin had been professor of homiletics to three generations of seminarians. Father Gilvary's class had been Glavin's last, and a fierce disappointment to him. In his final year of teaching, he'd expected, he'd hoped for "a feast of reason"; instead, all he'd gotten was "a flow of the usual."

Father Glavin had two funeral texts that served for all occasions: *I am the resurrection and the life* for the saved, and for dubious cases, or worse, the line from Second Maccabees: *It is a holy and wholesome thought to pray for the dead that they may be loosed from their sins.*

But, no, Father Gilvary would go a different route. He would use John's own words: "It'll be all right." And he has his text:

On the night He was betrayed, He gave thanks and praise.

The morning of the funeral is a checkerboard of cloud and sun. The rain comes in fistfuls, splattering the glass, then a burst of light.

The weather matches Father Gilvary's mood. In the sacristy, before vesting, he kneels down at the side of the casket for a moment and rests his hands on the lid. No words of prayer come to mind. He addresses John silently, admiringly, *You've gone the whole course . . . further than I . . .* If life is catechumenal, as Father Gilvary has been taught, then John has graduated into clarity and peace. If not . . . He calls to mind his last glimpses of John at the wake, before the coffin was closed, ruddy and carnal in death . . . If not?

As a young seminarian, Father Gilvary had asked himself with each new book, at each stage of initiation—acolyte, lector, keeper of the keys, exorcist, at the subdiaconate, stepping forth to proclaim *adsum* to a life of celibacy—will this be the book, the rite, the sacrament that makes me holy? That makes me sure? For nothing had changed, and slowly he learned that nothing would change. He was still what he had always been: himself: a creature among creatures. Never sure.

Now he asks only to be of use.

How much difference was there between himself and Raymond Torrey, say, or Sam Wells, or a host of others who left and were dispensed from their vows? Precious little, he suspects. Only a hairsbreadth of difference at first, then a widening difference. Stubborn, is all. He'd continued to wait upon the Spirit. Hour after hour, he stood at the same door and would not budge from it. Famished with expectation, he'd knocked and knocked–

He has formally met the coffin at the door of the church, greeted it with pall and holy water. These simple gestures, as always, turn the tide of feeling for Father Gilvary. Only the presence of the Knights of Columbus in full regalia is a jarring distraction. Yet the Knights have a perfect right to be here. John was one of their own and they are ready to escort him now, an honor guard, three at the head and three at the foot. One by one, their ranks are dwindling.

They put him in mind of Henrietta, the proprietress of Three Square Meals–those absurd eyelashes, the fevered hectic in her cheeks. Is it a masquerade? Or a great gallantry? He can never decide. With the Knights, it's the same question. There they stand, wizened, pale in their cocked plumes of gold and scarlet, their capes flung back so the brilliant satin lining shows. They'll put out an eye, he thinks, as they raise their thin swords.

At the pulpit, Father Gilvary picks up the little olive of a microphone. He crackles the pages of his notes, although he has little need for notes today.

Silence, but for a metallic, needle-thin shrieking from one of the middle rows. Hand on a hearing aid does that.

Time to begin. "It'll be all right. I'm ready for it, whatever it is, the next thing . . . ," Father Gilvary tells them of John's last words. How often has he, an ordained priest, found his own halting faith restored, given back to him by those who believed. *We walk by faith, not by sight—* how often has he preached that text, spoken of faith as the grace to walk forward in darkness as though it were light, to doubt and keep on walking. John had that grace.

"Out of your own pain, speak," Father Glavin had instructed him. "Fix your gaze on the choir loft. Imagine the risen Lord in the choir loft. Imagine Lazarus coming forward to meet you. Stop for a moment and relish the sight."

There is no one in the choir loft today. The faithful seven who sing at funerals are none too spry themselves, and Father Gilvary cannot bear to watch them toiling up and down the steps; he's positioned them down in front instead.

He fixes his gaze on the choir loft. The light is watery, unstable. Nothing to see up there but a mosaic of stained glass. A thing of patches. Saint Jude, intercessor for those in desperate straits, patron saint of lost causes, crowned with battleaxes—a man of patches, standing among thistles. His long arms are stretched out entreatingly to Father Gilvary; he seems to be beckoning: *Look here*– Then a sunburst shatters the frame–Saint Jude passes through the flaming wreckage as a man through an open door–and stands free, stands free!–intact, without a fracture, one body bound up and made whole.

In a moment, in the twinkling of an eye, everything is changed.

And back again. Must be clouds passing. The light has shifted, dimmed as suddenly as it brightened. There's a soft, patting sound of wind and rain against the glass. They are back to fragments.

Altogether too much upward gazing for Father Gilvary. It is time to move on.

After Communion and tidying up, Father Gilvary makes his way to the bench behind the altar and sits gratefully. For this moment of silence, much thanks. Silently, he speaks his last words to John, *Be seeing you* . . . He bathes his eyes in the milky white of the altar cloth, then, briefly, closes them.

All too briefly. He can hear one of the women in the choir whispering, "A mercy . . . a great mercy."

Already it is time to rise and bless the congregation. Time for the recessional, "Magnify the Name," sung brokenly at first, then with annealing force.

Face to Face

The door is locked but in the night he hears someone, barefoot, pacing the hall and, twice, the sound of a hand on the door, the doorknob turning–somebody testing.

It's broad day now and bed isn't restful, but Cleat is not yet ready to sit up and touch his feet down to the floorboards. He's floating somewhere between sleep and waking–asleep to the room, the street, the cars passing outside, but awake, awake and prowling, inside.

He's still in the car with Val. Only, this time, it is Val who's trapped and hurting and he, Cleat, who works himself free, then reaches in and touches Val where his shoulder is pinned under metal. "Val?" Val's skin is rough. Warm.

"Cleat?" Val's answering voice is like a knock on the door, that close. That clear. Val's lip is torn and gleaming with blood.

Cleat leans in and licks it off.

The paper shade rattles in a gust and Cleat opens his eyes. He rubs his forehead: it's still a little sore, the bruise is there, but the lump is down, the clawing headache is gone. So why not get up now? His day off—why waste it? He could play the same dream over and over, never tiring, never moving on.

It's a tight little room, a narrow space, angled to the morning sun, three stories up near the corner of Tyler and Line. The paint on the ceiling is cracking, and there's a hole in the wall of the closet that Cleat has stuffed up with a wad of toilet paper. Sometimes the voice came from that opening, but the last time Cleat went to it, there was no sound; fitting his eye to the hole, what he saw was the edge of the dresser in the room next door and a piece of the iron bedstead exactly like his own. Once, he found an eye, dark, staring back at him, but that never happened again.

Dresser, mirror, the steel frame of a chair, its thin padding knifed out, bed, closet—these are the furnishings in Cleat's room. He keeps most everything he values in a locked trunk under the bed. On the dresser is a comb and brush, Bible, stack of handouts—that's all. The handouts are a new bunch. He has printed the message in a very tiny hand:

IT IS THE LORD WHO

HAS TORN US ASUNDER

BUT HE WILL HEAL US

For the longest time Cleat's had a suspicion that someday his real father would come into Durance to take a look at him. To see how his son has turned out. His hair would be red, like Cleat's, but he'd stand in a doorway or behind a car, someplace where he could see without being seen, and Cleat would never know. Would never see his father's face. The man would stand there for a minute or two, just looking, keeping his thoughts to himself, then pass on through.

The voice first came to Cleat when he was thinking of his father. He was working at Toot n' Totum; it must of been two or three in the morning. The pinball machines were humming and clacking to empty air: there hadn't been a customer in a long while.

The voice was not especially loud or impressive. It seemed to be coming from the old cash register. It said—it sounded like—"Start walking." Or "Star walking." Cleat wasn't sure. Later, the messages were clearer. He wishes he could recall what those first words were exactly. Could of been, "Stop wanting."

When Cleat steps out into the street, the light is all around him. Hot as blazes and still early. He pauses under the awning of Tibbett's Bridal for a spot of shade. Free to go anywhere, Cleat cannot think where. Post office? Restaurant? There's no one to tell him where to go. A woman in a red bandanna goes by, legs scissoring fast, and he starts after her, trailing, one step, then another, watching his feet move like they belonged to somebody else. Must be something doing wherever she's going.

He's disappointed when, only a few blocks up the way, the woman disappears into a grocery store. But

Cleat keeps on walking the way he's been heading: the K Mart is open; he's thought of something.

The booth is in back, near the hardware. Right where he thought:

NO WAITING—INSTANT LIKENESS

Seventy-five cents now. Cleat rummages in his pockets for quarters, then enters the photomatic booth. There are two curtains for backdrop: one blue, one yellow —one shady, one sunny. Cleat decides on blue. He sits, then notices the eye level marker is too low and stands up to gear the stool down. Three twirls does the trick.

Now he folds his glasses into his pocket, spit-combs his hair and smooths his eyebrows with a finger. He smiles for practice, pouts to unfreeze the smile, moistens the corners of his lips.

Forgotten anything?

No. He's about ready. Ready as he ever will be. He stares into the little window facing him, down through the glass into the deep, blinkered eye he knows is hiding there. Soon as he drops the third quarter, the machine starts making noises. A click: Now. Look serious. Now: Smile. And now: Turn, just a—

Now he'll see. A sign flashes—PLEASE WAIT OUTSIDE—so he steps out and stands by the delivery slot.

They're not all that bad, but it's clear he should of kept his glasses on, his eyes are too squinty. The third photo, the one where he turned, is missing half—half of his face lost in a smear of motion. The second photo, the smiling one, is best, but he still looks like a kid in it. The strongest thing in any one of the pictures is the curtain

Face to Face

back of his head, falling in folds so sharp and stiff they might be hacked in wood.

Seven minutes to go. Val is in the middle of his break. He's trying to make a list, sitting at the booth farthest from the door so maybe he can concentrate. The place is empty, except for one of the customers standing near the register. She settled her bill some minutes back, but she's still hanging around, yukking it up with Henrietta. Complaining how she can never get a haircut she likes.

"That's funny, Shelly," says Henrietta. "Seeing as you're a beauty operator yourself."

"Wish I could take my head off and set it on a platter and cut my own hair. Nobody does it right. I've had the same customers sixteen years and they all say, 'Shelly—' "

Val has it figured out. Everybody is acting at Three Square Meals. Shelly's acting the beauty operator, and Henrietta's doing her favorite thing, her bartender-psychiatrist listening act. Stella is playing Cinderella. And the next people to walk through the door will be playing customers with walk-on parts.

He hopes business doesn't pick up too soon, since everything—everything!—is coming back to him now. Total recall. The lawyers are droning away, the judge murmuring, then everyone's shouting at once. He's standing at the ear of a wind tunnel, feels like. He hears his own voice, the diminished echo of his voice, piping into this ferocious wind of words. He has an objection—are only lawyers allowed to object? It's *his* case, after all, he hired the lawyer, brought the suit, cost him plenty. *Objection!*

193

He's been robbed–twice–there's a law, isn't there a law?
He worked, slaved for years to buy those things. He's
been dragged through the mud; they're all a bunch of
crooks–the judge, his lawyer, her lawyer, the witness for
the insurance company, the art appraiser calling his collection "junk," all the flunkeys of the court!

Ignore them, tune them out–get on with the list–
FEMALE MUSICIANS (ORIENTAL, RED AND GOLD)
They were on black, black velvet; it's so clear now.
BOY WITH FRUIT BASKET (OILS)
That was in the foyer.
BLUE & GREEN FEMALE NUDE
Keep writing. But the voices are louder now, closer.
The hammer you don't recall?
Your Honor, I object!
Strike it from the record. That was never said.
*What was the first thing you did when you came into
the apartment and saw the paintings were gone? Do you
recall? Do you want a moment to refresh your recollection?*
Objection!
Keep on writing. BLUE & GREEN . . . got that already.
Ignore them. Forget it–what they said, he said, she said, he
said, it's all wind. Forget what you said–you were pro-
voked.

But the voices aren't stopping.
*Objection overruled. You have an exception. Proceed.
The first thing you did, please.*
*My wife had just left me—I felt like my corpuscles were
coming apart!*
*The court is not interested in your feelings. She wasn't
your wife.*

*She'd run off with a crook, they came in like a bunch of
animals. They cleaned me out—*

And what did you do to her before she ran off?

Nothing.

Did you hold a hammer to her head?

I don't recall.

*Threatening to bash her brains out did not impress itself
sufficiently upon your mind to—*

*Your Honor, I object! This is a suit for the restitution of
property.*

Strike it from the record.

Keep writing. BLUE & GREEN—No, no, how many
times? In the living room, what else?

CLOWN ON BALCONY

SILK SCREEN IN GOLD FRAME

As clear as day: the silk screen was over the stereo. It
was beautiful.

Who's this? Somebody standing in his light, crowd-
ing him. Cleat, who else, another handout.

"Not now," says Val. "Can't you see I'm busy?" And
he bends over his list.

Cleat seems to freeze in place. Henrietta calls over
does he want a Coke, but gets no answer.

"Stop breathing down my neck," says Val.

SILK SCREEN IN GOLD FRAME

The silk screen was over the stereo. *The living room
was all disheveled, all dissolved, everything was gone from the
walls, I remember that—*

*Your memory is very selective. The hammer you don't
recall?*

Objection!

Your Honor, if this man persists in his suit, my client will run him up on a charge of criminal assault.

Objection!

I'm going to hold you both in contempt if you continue–

I know one thing– The silk screen was over the stereo. It was beautiful. *I loved what I bought.*

Nobody listens. They're standing in a huddle at the judge's bench, his lawyer and hers, their backs to him. He's walking out, slamming doors. But those doors don't slam, they sigh: *erase it from the record . . . that was never said . . .* Down the hallway, he shouts, he doesn't care now– out of the courthouse, out of the city, out–

It broke my heart.

IN GOLD FRAME . . . A shadow muddies the page. It's Cleat. He's boxing Val in. "Can't you see I'm busy?" Val says without looking up. "Quit hassling me!" And he presses the pencil so hard that the point snaps.

Why won't he clear off? Stands there like a statue, another one of those messages from Mars in his hand. "Get lost," says Val. Cleat reaches out and aims the thing flat smack over where Val's been writing.

And Val lashes back: "Shut up, shut up, shut up!"

At that, Cleat lets go and stumbles to the door.

A Precaution

Henrietta was watching as Val tore the photos–sight unseen–into shreds, then swept the clutter off the table with a fast swipe of his hand. And not into the ashtray, mind you, but onto the floor. Then he went right on sitting there, ticking off some kind of inventory, some kind of list. Treasuring up wrath. One way or another, he was asking for it. She wanted to tell him: we forgive because we have been forgiven.

But she still wasn't sure what his problem was. "You better get a broom," is all she said.

He answered by moving his lips. Though no sound came out, she knew what the words were. They fell like gobs of mud.

Shutupshutupshutup!

What to do? It gets Henrietta so nervous watching him her toes tighten and clench up. She can't fire him; he works too hard. But she'll have to be watchful. She'd seen a couple of his lists—short ones—he's been trying for a long time, making starts and breaking off. They're about paintings and money, as far as she can judge. She wants to tell him about money: know how much a dollar's worth? Two tenths of a cent. Know how much a ten-thousand-dollar bill is worth? Two tenths of a cent.

She wants to warn him about living in little things, how King Ahab had a palace in Jezreel, all laid up in ivory, nicest you'd ever want to see, and how he wanted only what he didn't have—a little garden. How Naboth had a vineyard hard by it that would make a garden, and everything from that vineyard was bitter to Ahab. Though he was a king, he lived in little things. She'd like to tell Val that. But you can't really talk to Val without permission, an opening, a chink in what looks to be a solid wall he's stacked up around him. So all Henrietta says is, once again, "You better clean that up before the next customer comes in."

Henrietta has Val on her mind nearly all the time now. She knows that Stella hankers after Val, and she and Stella both know that it will come to nothing. Stella can look out for herself. It's that other one that's really got her worried—that sad, lost shadow of a boy, Cleat. Wouldn't know his own name except it was pinned to him.

Most everybody feels how lost he is. "I wouldn't know the sound of him," Honeybun Chesem keeps saying.

"In my whole life, I never heard his voice. Is he simple, you think?"

"You could call him anything else–'locked-in,' maybe –but not simple," is Henrietta's answer to that. "Isn't a soul in town–not Buck nor Betty, and they're closest– been able to figure him out. You read his notices? I mean, really read them?"

There are some things you know even before they happen, or, right after, you know you should of known before. Like watching a toddler spill a glass of milk: you see it in your mind's eye beforehand, you see it in slow motion while it's happening–you clap your hands, *hold it, right there!*—and it happens. Because you said to yourself beforehand: *plenty of time. Time enough to do something when the time comes.* Count on it: it comes. Like the last visit Ma made to Durance; on the day she arrived, she said, "I'll be leaving on the twentieth." Henrietta thought she meant that she'd be returning to Wayside on the twentieth. Ma was in good health at the time, just the best of spirits. A week later, she took the flu, then pneumonia, and on the twentieth of November she died.

Henrietta never would forget that day. She'd come back from lunch–it was clear then that Ma couldn't hold on much longer. Henrietta had only been gone a couple of hours, but soon as she stepped into the bedroom Ma said, "Where were you all this while? I've been home to Wayside and back. The strangest thing . . . When I got home I found the door wide open–"

In her mind, she'd gone home. She knew.

Something's coming. Soon. It's bound to. And Henrietta knows it's not going to be pretty. Knowing's not going to make a particle of difference, though. Only the other day, she'd read about a man in the paper who'd leaped to his feet in his motorboat, hollering, "Here I am!" —when the lightning forked down and sizzled him on the spot. Fried him to a crisp. Out of a nice blue sky!

He knew. It didn't change a thing.

It's been a slow day. The slowest in living memory, she's tempted to say, but her memory mustn't be too sharp, because she's had that thought many a time before. She's been sitting at this table forever, it seems, waiting for time to pass.

Outside, the dark is coming down inch by inch. Val's day off, so Stella is rolling the cart up and down between the tables, taking up the dirty dishes. Leroy is the only customer left. He's dawdling over his half-eaten plate like it's his last meal in all the world. Sits there, head propped on elbows, his hat resting between the napkin holder and the hot sauce. It's rare to see him in public with his hat off. There's a permanent indentment over his eyebrows, a red line that shows where it goes, that hat is so wedded to his head. He's been brooding on something, or praying over it, no telling what. There's ketchup in the corners of his lips and a dab of red on his chin. Eats ketchup on everything.

"There you go again," says Stella.

"Ma'am?"

"You're not going to eat your carrots?"

Leroy stares glumly at his plate and tries to explain how he has no use for vegetables–"None of them things that grows in the ground."

Then Stella lifts Leroy's platter, holding it aloft like

a prize exhibit. She picks up his fork and pokes it around the platter. "Plenty of good fish left!" she says.

"Ma'am?"

"That's a good fish. Comes all the way from Galveston. He can't be caught again!"

Henrietta doesn't know what gets into Stella sometimes. On the prod, since morning. She started out by spilling a trayful of dishes at breakfast, breaking a couple, and somebody clapped and somebody called out, "Way to go, Stell!" By noon, she was jumpy as a wet hen. Henrietta heard her slapping down an order of hot dogs for five, saying "A dog for you!–a dog for you!" Five times. And now, nagging at Leroy, such a good customer and the nicest man.

"You may not be smart, Stella, but you can be quiet," Henrietta scolds. She's amazed to hear herself–Ma's very words leaping from her own lips.

Stella bumps the cart along to the kitchen, making as rackety a clatter as she can. And now all you can hear is the sound of water going full force. Let her scour the demons out of her–

It takes the longest while, though. Henrietta kills time by filling up the sugar dispensers and the salt shakers. When she sees the lights in the kitchen go out, she calls over: "Stell–I'd like to visit with you a minute." And Stella comes out, flipping her hair.

"You're getting mighty pert, mighty mouthy," Henrietta says. "Can I know why?"

She doesn't answer right away, but stands there, picking at a stain on her sleeve. "He's bugging me," she answers finally.

"Who, Leroy?"

"Not him. Oh, you know. Why doesn't he go back where he comes from? He's not from Columbus, that was his first story–a bunch of bull. He's not from Ohio, but he's come a long ways to be here, and he's not really here– his mind's always somewheres else. Why'd he come?" Her voice is shaky, she's close to tears. "Do you know? Does he have a family someplace? Like, a mom? Girlfriend? Wife, you think? Anything! Maybe a dog? He never says blip about them. Ask him a friendly question and he goes deaf, stone deaf. Ever notice that? I can't imagine him needing anybody, ever. So why'd he come? What's he want here? It bugs me–"

After Stella goes, Henrietta lingers on for a few minutes more. There's no hurry. She isn't thinking of anything in particular, only staring, not taking much in.

She's staring on a slant. What her eyes can't seem to focus on is right smack in front of them: the prize knives hanging on the wall from the A-1 Cooking School in Letsem City. Little by little, those crossed knives have her complete attention. Can't decide. One part of her says: *no hurry. Think about it later.* The other says: *later may be too late.*

No, she's made up her mind. She'll take the knives down and hang them in her own kitchen at home. Out of harm's way. It's the best course. She can't keep the steak knives locked up, but she can keep from waving them in Val's face every time he comes in through the door.

It's a low season. Everybody restless, hankering after one thing or another. Only last week, Ellen Knighton, the cook at Fong's Golden Skillet, saw the Virgin Mary in her frying pan. Henrietta read about it in the newspaper first. What was the word they used?–an "apparel"?–"ap" what?–"appetition"? A fancy word, three-kerneled, as Henrietta recalls, some something of the "Holy Virgin," an appearing of some kind. Just however it was that the Romans talked was how the newspaper wrote it down.

After that, Ellen had refused to fry anything, only boil, and when Fong threatened to fire her, she'd phoned the newspaper and told them her story. And all week long the reporters kept coming, in and out of Fong's restaurant, one of them hailing from as far away as Oklahoma City. Asking questions everywhere. To Father Gilvary first, of course. "The Mother of God in a frying pan?" was what they said he said. He didn't sound all that keen on it. "And what is that supposed to mean to us?" he'd asked. Didn't sound at all sure what the answer might be. "That Mrs. Knighton's labor is blessed? Of course it is. Maybe the best miracle is Ellen Knighton thinking about the Queen of Heaven while working in a hot kitchen all day long."

And Brother Shad called it "popish mischief," though Ellen Knighton said she wasn't with the Romans anymore. She'd gone charismatic–Church of the Open Door–it's a new one. They have their own services over in Letsem City.

Sam Plemons let it be known that, in his opinion, the whole story was nothing but a way of drumming up some free advertising for Fong's Golden Skillet. And the reporters pestered Fong, asking him why he'd chosen the name "Golden Skillet" for the restaurant in the first place. Mightn't he of had some stunt like this in mind from the start? But Fong made it clear that, as a Baptist of sixteen years in good standing, he had no dealings with idols. FROWNING FONG was what they'd printed under his picture.

By now the fuss has pretty much died down. Ellen Knighton is frying on another skillet, not saying where she took the glorified one. Some people think she's sold it. Like Brother Shad said: "Mischief, no miracles" . . . it's a low season. Henrietta has her low blood, usual around this time of year. Brother Shad, too, is feeling skimped on enthusiasm lately. Didn't take long for the word to spread about him and Sister Willodene, how it came to nothing. "I prayed over it and I prayed over it," Brother Shad admitted. "I prayed up a whirlwind. But the devil set his foot against it, I couldn't pray her in."

The devil's underfoot, that's all there is to it. Some kind of webworm in things.

All Souls

For two days before the end of the month, the wind came out of the west–dry and sandy, and warm; for two days, the wind came out of the north, and it was wet and biting cold. On the next day, November had started, but it was as if summer had begun, blue, breathless and still. The cottonwoods were gold with summer light. The winter wheat had begun to stool out and cover the fields with new green.

Normally, at the approach of autumn or any change of season, Father Gilvary wove a theme around the weather. And the weather cooperated. The weather was his favorite text, capable of many small variations and elaborations. It had not failed him before this. In autumn and winter, he liked to say that the dying of the year was not the dying of hope, the sleep of nature was but a sleep, a drawing inward, a time of preparation. But nothing around him supported the theme of autumn so far. The mood of nature was, by turns, furious and festive. Nothing was tucking down and deepening; everything seemed to be whirling.

On the night between All Saints and All Souls, sleep eludes Father Gilvary. He can hear something, or some-one, breathing over him, the sound of rinsing, sighs and broken answers. "This one's the blacksmith," the words are mixed with the sound of generous pouring. "And this" –a few short splashes–"is his little helper." It's his father toasting births, baptisms, wakes, paydays, friendships, any and all anniversaries, glass after glass, until he's toasted each and every one of the thirty-two counties in Ireland.

Father Gilvary smiles into his pillow at the recollec-tion. How strange, to be smiling after all the years of bitterness–his sisters afraid to bring friends to the house, and his own flight to the seminary in a rage of piety.

Recollection is his burden for the day of All Souls, with a Mass at Saint Jude's and a visit to the cemetery on his schedule. A day for hovering souls, a day of healing for all those scraps of memory that throng the air, to bind them and lay them to rest.

Years ago, when Father Gilvary was a boy, Purga-tory had been something quite literally meant. He'd thought of it as a terrible traffic jam, the great bridge packed with travelers, a rush hour crowd, stalled–the air above it choked with cries. There was nothing metaphoric about Purgatory back then, none of these latter-day state-of-mind or healing-of-memory understandings. You had to pray people loose from that bridge. And you earned the release of souls as you earned your spending money. For each five Our Father's, five Hail Mary's, and five Glory Be's, one soul would pass through. Was it five? Or six? He no longer remembers the equation. He prayed up a storm, though, all the children of Saint Boniface did; they'd competed to see who could free the greatest number.

Today his gospel reading is from Saint John:

> *Now the will of Him who sent me*
> *is that I should lose nothing*
> *of all that He has given to me*
> *and that I should raise it up on the last day*

Father Gilvary would speak of the divine economy, in which the dead are near, silenced only by our terror of them, in which our prayers are letters, and our letters are never lost.

There were days when he fully believed this, and days when he wished desperately to believe it. And there were days when he found it flat out impossible to believe it, when God's creation seemed the kind of letter that the writer never touched. Dictated and dispatched; signed in his absence. Garbled in transmission.

While All Saints is a holy day of obligation and well attended, All Souls is merely a solemn commemoration, and the crowd at Saint Jude's is much attenuated. Then only a remnant of that morning crowd joins Father Gilvary at the cemetery in the afternoon.

Father Gilvary is a little early. He busies himself by roaming the grounds. The dead are very close to him today, and present things strangely far. From where he stands, the Interstate looks to him like smoke unwinding, dissolving in sky. His vision is partial now–here, a double printing of grass and stone: light fits a helmet to the stone and stencils with thin gold the borders of each leaf; there, like a thumbprint, a smudge of ash against a clean sweep of sky; an erasure over there, where a segment of hedge– he blinks to give it another chance–has been quietly, entirely, omitted.

Only a minute or two more to wander.

A low hedge, serving also as a windbreak, separates the Catholic dead from the Protestant. Reaching the out-ermost circle of Catholic stones, Father Gilvary spies a fallen wreath, then, coming closer, a bird nesting in its plastic leaves. Really, the upkeep–

And here's something he'll have to speak to the office about–a clear case of vandalism. Someone's been out here spray painting the stones. Father Gilvary stoops and extends his finger to the one that says JESUS COME–to make sure he's not dreaming. No, it's real: the paint is fresh, black, still wet, flaked with bird lime. Here's a stone that says STONE SPEAK, and, on the one next to it, the name ALRED is scrawled over with three words:

ARMS OF VAPOR

Leaning closer, Father Gilvary spies someone crouching in the hedge. It's Cletus, he's almost sure, the boy from the post office.

And now he's running–a blotch–a blot of fear against the empty sky. Father Gilvary turns abruptly. He must think about this, but later. It's time to return to his own group. The canopy is up, he'd best get back over.

When he scans the horizon again, there is no one to be seen. The light is strange: gold, then gray remembering gold, a dreamy light.

The spray paint was real, though.

Father Gilvary stands under the canopy, his parishioners in a straggling circle around him. What he must say is clear to him.

"One dies, and then another," he directs his voice over the hedge. "The connection still holds. The connection survives us. We are bound in the one net. Our prayers are letters, and no letters are ever lost. No love is ever wasted."

He believes this. Or wants so much to believe it that it comes to the same thing.

But the cemetery is deserted. Except for the delegation from Saint Jude, no one is visiting the graves today. The trees stand, swaying restlessly, and the stones deafly attentive.

Smoke and Stone

Jerkwater town! A cattle truck, bumping down the street, throws off mud, hair, manure and hay in its wake. The cattle are packed tight, rubbing their hides raw against the metal slats. A moony eye, framed by slats, regards Val. Follows him–speakingly.

Gotta get out of here!

There are no accidents: everything's aimed, aimed at getting to Val. He hears a stealthy footfall, faintly echoing his own. He knows who that will be, and, turning with sharp, neck-wrenching suddenness, cries: "Get lost!"

A great mistake–his calling out is a summons, the footfall louder, closer now. What follows is not what he thought. Nothing but a mean, lean yellow bitch with a winking eye.

"Get lost!"

Her ears lift. She follows with steady persistence, knocking into his shins and whimpering. Hungry, collarless, her hair matted and damp.

Val walks on faster.

Behind him, a steady, dry plashing. Then a burst of speed. Now she runs parallel to Val, her pace matching his.

Rushing in front, she crashes into Val's left shin; then, slowing precipitously, dips behind him, knocking him on the right. There is no way, short of kicking her, that Val can break out of her noose.

She hasn't got a collar—no rabies shot to tell of— that's all that keeps him from kicking her to kingdom come.

Cleat makes his way down Travis Street. A cattle truck clatters by, and a stray dog who weaves around him for two whole blocks, shaky, running to keep from falling, looks like, then drops behind. The air is quick with changes, the cottonwoods going from yellow to brown. The leaves are falling. They fall and fly up. There's a hard rain coming, he's sure.

He's learned some hard things this year, so far.

Be smoke or stone, that's one thing he learned. There is no middle way. Be hard and sealed, or loose and soft and almost invisible—then people pass clear through you, like air. Like smoke. Cleat is tired of being smoke. He wants to be stone—like Val.

He turns when he comes to the cemetery. The sight of the grass so faded with sun makes him thirsty. Sleepy, too. Last night, he dreamed about the cemetery; he was running, a man with a big staple gun was calling to him, a man in a black suit, stapling leaves to a hedge. Cleat kept on running.

But here it is: THREE SQUARE MEALS.

"He called her 'honey?' "

"Yes. And that's how I knew how angry he was."

The voices wash around Henrietta, not making much sense. She's had enough harassments in the past few hours to last her the whole week. Round about ten, this straggly girl with a backpack came in for a cup of coffee. Filthy, and eyeing the truckers, so Henrietta figured she must of been a hitchhiker, or worse. She was wearing this sweatshirt that had FRIEND printed loud across it, though she looked like she hadn't a friend in the world. After she left, Henrietta found the toilet bowl stuffed with paper towels.

And now, in the very same booth, there sits the Roman piddling over his coffee, his collar unhinged. Hasn't said "boo" to anybody since he came in. Val's surly with him, swishing his cleanup rag over the table with the old man still sitting there.

But Val's short with everybody today and, soon as Cleat steps through the door, Henrietta knows there's trouble in the air. She can feel Val's rage, slow but building steady, starting to boil, everything in his path starting to shake with it. She thinks: He wants to kill what's killed him. If he can find it.

In a minute she's going to dispatch him. But–where to? Send him back to the kitchen. Or, better yet, out to the alley to stash the garbage. Tomorrow is pickup day, though, usually, she waits for evening to put it out.

Henrietta's just about to send him back there when she overhears something about Brother Shad and Sister Willodene, something so foul it makes her toes curl, and she gets sidetracked. Word sure travels. How that story takes a sprout with every telling! She simply has to put her foot down before it grows out of all recognition.

When she's done setting the facts straight and glances Val's way again, what she feared has already begun.

Something she's not meant to see: Cleat is talking, low and serious the way he does, gazing up into Val's face –may the Lord protect us from what we love!–and Val's biting back whatever he might say, his lips pressed white, he's not even looking at the boy, too busy scribbling on his order pad. He presses the pencil hard and Henrietta knows it's not an order he's taking down. It's a note, and she's plumb certain it's nasty.

There's a glass of ice water standing on the counter between them. Untouched, except for the place where Cleat's finger has stroked two clear lines in the clouded glass.

Two clear lines . . . Val, Cleat.

And Cleat sitting there with his face tilted up to Val, asking only, *Look at me–call my name–* Henrietta can't bear to watch it. She moves forward with one word echoing in her head: *Don't.* But not stopping for it.

Flumps herself right down in the middle of it, saying to Val, "I'll take that order. I want you to go back into the kitchen and put the garbage out. Hear? Right now!"

Val doesn't so much as glance up from his scribbling.

"This minute," Henrietta keeps on. "You hear me? You have ears?"

Val slides the order slip in between the ketchup and the napkin dispenser before taking off. Cleat's nimble–plucks it right out.

"You know about our special today?" is the only thing Henrietta can think of to say to the boy. Anything to get him to lift his head, to unstick him from that note.

"Don't suppose I can interest you in some coconut custard pie?"

But he's already on his feet, hurrying to the kitchen after Val. Punching the swing doors so hard they go back and forth three times–

And Henrietta must see to the man waiting at the register. "Careful, gal, that's my last," he says, handing over a ten. "After this, I go on welfare." She has to wait there while he counts the change down to the last penny, then studies the chewing tobacco in the glass case like he's fixing to buy one brand or another. " 'Less I win a lottery," he says, "I sure could use to win," when Henrietta hears this terrific whanging and banging.

Everybody hears it. The Roman stumbles to his feet.

"Be back in no time!" Henrietta calls as she hurries by, thinking he, too, is headed for the cash register, but, no, he just stands there, crossing himself and listening. In the kitchen, the radio's going—there's this great long blurt of static.

"That's some wind," Stella says, fussing with the dial.

Henrietta knows it isn't the wind.

Nothing blowing in the alley but the dust. There's rain in the air.

Where are they?

The dumpster lid is up and, right away, Henrietta is lost in annoyance about that. Where's Val? She's told him time and time again how the wind takes things. You've got to keep that lid down—no "if," "and," or "maybe" about it! She slams down the lid and— What was that?

Hears something.

This thin, dull thudding against metal. Something live, some animal, trapped inside. She lifts the lid, slowly, and leans over the rim.

Something down there too big to throw away.

Cleat. Like she's known all along.

He's crumpled up into a ball and his face is dark with blood. His foot is beating against the metal siding, that's how she knows he's alive.

That's when she starts hollering.

Morning Again

Val was within hailing distance, but running hard, when Henrietta arrived at the dumpster. By the time she'd figured out what happened, he was well on his way to the open road.

On the Interstate, he hitches a ride on a semi bound for Tucumcari. No time to pack up, but he has his wallet—which is most of what he owns. He'll be traveling light.

The driver doesn't talk much once they near the state line. "Take any exit"–there's an ad on the radio for a restaurant in Santa Rosa.

"No way to get lost.
Plenty of parking.
Follow fat face . . ."

Already, Durance is a bad dream. Val's riding high in the cab, feeling lighter and lighter as the miles fly by. Why did he ever stay? It had something to do with a sunset. He pulled off his suitcase and stayed, stuck around so long it seems like years. Then things really closing in at the end.

He's moving on. On past the spikes of milo stubble, the leave-out land, the feedlots, out on to prairie rusty with autumn light. He's been needing to shake loose for some time.

From Tucumcari, he'll hop a bus to L.A. Where he'd been heading before. He's never been to L.A., a big city is what he needs now.

He's on his way!

He's primed for it. It's something big and bright he's feeling, warm on the outside, cool on the inside. The farther he goes from anywhere he's been before, the brighter it gets.

This was his obedience, his faith perhaps—rising to meet his eight o'clock through every mood and weather. The daily sacrament of bread—thanking, offering, breaking, giving. *Do this in memory of Me.* Meeting the dwindling few who showed up for daily Mass morning after morning, keeping faith, answering faithfulness with faithfulness. Being here, a light in the house, a voice, a hand, an ear, for whoever came. And if no one came—still, being here.

The chill startles him: the floorboards as he touches his feet down, the sill as he lifts the shade, like a thin slick of frost on everything. Gray light. The facing tree is still dark.

"Where are you?"

Winter's on its way. Advent. Beginning again: the year swings round to its renewal of expectation. This Sunday coming up, the solemnity of Christ the King, will be the last Sunday in ordinary time.

The pierced, the tattered king.

It is time to speak to the bishop. Father Gilvary is now legally blind. Of course, Dr. Stas assured him, many people lead normal lives even though legally blind. "But," he added, "your case will not rest there."

Tuus est dies, et tua est nox . . .

Nothing rests, but Father Gilvary lingers in the empty church long after the Mass has ended. He remains in an attitude of prayer, on his knees, his lips moving soundlessly although he cannot pray. He summons all the words yet cannot lift them. There is nothing in him but the longing to pray, sharp as a thorn. He offers it up. He says simply, as he answered *adsum* to that first roll call, "I'm here." Asks: "Be with me now."

Shadows throng the walls, closer every time. He turns his face to the sanctuary lamp. Still there. Red-eyed, sleepless, still burning.

Morning again.

There are days when Henrietta does not want to stir from her bed. This sure is one of them. The chillier it gets the less inclined she is to leave the warm cave she's made for herself. And it won't be getting any easier. Come sixty, she figures, people either curl in or unfold. Choose one.

"That's how Laodicea got its trip to the lake of fire!"

Henrietta twirls the radio dial on past Brother Ames, trying to hunt up some marching music. Only thing she finds is this sudden, sad little spasm of song, new, yet familiar. "If I'd met you twenty years before . . . Yooo're once in a blue million . . ." Wailing away. She's heard a hundred songs like it, about what might of been, what once almost nearly came to be. It's Maybe-land. I could live there, she tells herself, but I won't. Out from under! Come on, let's go— But she's not budging yet.

Somebody has to open up. Got to keep things going. She thinks of the early stragglers coming in out of the cold in search of their warming cups. Somebody has to be there for them. So she reaches for her terry-cloth robe bunched at the foot of the bed, reminding herself that it's time to dig out the woolen one. Out of her covers, it's shocking cold, it shakes her with a last-leaf-on-the-tree feeling—but she's on her way. First to wash up. Then, with care, to put on her face.

Oh, smile—smile, who wants such a sourpuss?

Weather's the main topic of conversation at the restaurant this morning, how the cold season's starting early. There's still more than a week of November to go, and here they all are in heavy coats—some in hats and gloves, even.

What happened between Cleat and Val has pretty much been talked out by now. It's a real sad thing and, while Henrietta doesn't dwell on it, she doesn't forget, either. Poor lost boy . . . to see so little under so wide a sky. To plant your hope in such stony ground! Val was stony ground. Not even that. Nothing so steady as ground, nothing but a wind, a mean, cold wind, blowing in and blowing out the way he came–

Everything about him was cold: cold anger, cold calm.

Father Gilvary rode along with Cleat in the ambulance, but when Betty and Buck got news of it they asked the doctor to keep all visitors away. They didn't trust the Romans, and couldn't say so in plain words, so they ended up locking everybody out.

Henrietta picked up the details from here and there. Heard how he'd lain in a coma three, four hours, then opened his eyes and spoke his first words:

"Shut up, shut up, shut up–"

Two days later he was gone, cleared out of the hospital without permission. One of the truckers who stopped by at Henrietta's on a regular route thought he'd seen a boy with his head wrapped up hitching a ride with a driver who worked out of Denver, but he couldn't swear that the kid he remembered matched the picture of the boy in the newspaper. Anyhow, there was no saying where that boy might be by now, since Denver's a junction for all points.

The sheriff followed Val's trail to a truck stop in Tucumcari, then lost it. There weren't any warrants out on him from any other state–at least, nothing turned in yet.

See how they run.

Seems like everybody's leaving. And Henrietta

knows—not how or when, but soon—that Brother Shad, too, will be moving on.

And here she is.

Henrietta sits at one of the front tables, sorting forks, knives and spoons into bunches. There's a sign in the window; she's still short on help. It's between breakfast and lunch, a slow time. Father Gilvary is the only customer left; he's dawdling and warming his hands round his cup, even blowing on it from time to time, out of habit. It can't be very warm by now. He doesn't want another refill, though; she offered. Doesn't seem in any hurry to be out in the weather. Words come to her: *a tired yet listening heart* . . . Listening so hard she can hear him. When she drops a knife and it skitters against the linoleum, he looks up suddenly, staring a little to the side of where it fell, and keeps on staring. He's got that way of leaning too long after the light that tells her he's blinder than he was.

It's quiet now. Henrietta is full of thoughts, full of wonderment. Here they are, herself and the Roman, having nothing in the world to say to one another, but sharing this slow time, alive in the day together. They aren't rushing on to the next thing, they aren't even waiting on the next thing.

And if Jesus were to arrive this very minute, she's ready. *Just as I am.* Ready as she'll ever be.

Henrietta is done waiting—done dwelling in some other time, past or yet to come. There've been so many disappointments, though that isn't why. She's had her share of things, too. Not her fill, but her share. It's restful to think she can settle on that.

Then, wouldn't you know it, just when she's settling into a kind of peacefulness, somebody—Russ Bearden—storms in. In a tearing hurry—not a minute to spare. He's lost a pair of gloves.

"A whole pair?" says Henrietta.

There's nothing whole in the lost-and-found box as far as she recalls, but better check to make sure.

"No—not here." It's all bits and pieces, like she thought. A loose ChapStick, and a kid's mitten that's been around since last winter. A blue button earring. A key chain with only one key on it.

"We don't have two of anything here," she calls over to Russ. But glancing back at the old man dawdling there, dreaming into his empty cup—soon as she's said it—she knows it isn't true.

About the Author

Since leaving New York seven years ago, A. G. Mojtabai *has lived on the High Plains of Texas and has been a close student of Bible Belt culture. Her nonfiction book* Blessed Assurance *won the Lillian Smith Award as the best book about the American South in 1986. She has written four previous novels—*Mundome, The Yoo Eels of Sigmund Freud, A Stopping Place, *and received an award from the American Academy and Institute of Arts and Letters for her fourth novel,* Autumn.

Ms. Mojtabai has taught at Hunter College, New York University, and Harvard. Currently, she teaches at the University of Tulsa in Oklahoma.

BOOK MARK

The text of this book was composed in
the typeface Caslon Old Style
with the display in Canterbury
by Berryville Graphics,
Berryville, Virginia

It was printed on 55 lb. Glatfelter
by Berryville Graphics,
Berryville, Virginia
ORNAMENTATION AND DESIGN
BY CAROL MALCOLM